BIRTH OF THE ENGLISH

ENGLISH

Wallis Peel

CHIVERS

British Library Cataloguing in Publication Data available

This Large Print edition published by AudioGo Ltd, Bath, 2011.
Published by arrangement with the Author

U.K.   Hardcover   ISBN   978 1 445 83830 4
U.K.   Softcover   ISBN   978 1 445 83831 1

Printed and bound in Great Britain by
MPG Books Group Limited

For

Christine Ann Bassett née Tebb of
Montana, USA and York, UK

ONE

He stood before her feeling so dreadful and upset but managed to force tears away. He wore a short red and blue cloak to denote his superior rank, short breeches of a dun colour, hose cross-gartered and feet clad in fine leather boots. On his left hip he proudly carried a tiny sword, on his right was his eating dagger.

'Why, Aunt?' he asked plaintively.

Aethelflaeda, the Lady of Mercia, eyed him as her heart throbbed for him. He was so young and this was his very first devastating shock. Almost too much for his five years. How could she explain without giving more hurt?

'Why has Mother been thrown aside and why have I been sent to live with you, Aunty?'

The latter bit was easy to answer. 'But you know, Aethelstan, that all children go into another person's home for their education. It is the custom,' she told him gently.

He thought about that for a brief instant. 'But why Mother . . .?' He halted as realisation dawned. 'It's because Father did not marry her so now he's getting a proper wife to have sons from her. Because I'm just a bastard!'

There was nothing she could reply to this truthful statement but she silently cursed her tactless and cruel brother. There was little

1

love lost between them because Edward was crippled with jealousy about her. She knew she was her father's favourite and the eldest because it was to her he had always turned first, and again she knew why. Brother Edward was a fine warrior with physical courage. She could not dispute that, but he lacked her tactical flair for all matters military. Matters had to be spelled out to Edward, whereas she could see, in a flash, the pros and cons of a situation like her gallant father, King Alfred, now referred to as the Great. Even when her father had arranged her marriage she had always sat in on conference matters. This had annoyed her husband, which bothered her not one iota. There was nothing he could say or do to the great Alfred's daughter, and the men all listened to her opinions. She rode into battle with them, at their head, and how the Danes hated her. It took only a little time for her to be referred to as The Lady, and when she appeared every warrior would quiver with anticipation to leap to her bidding.

Edward writhed with jealousy. This made her uneasy for the fate of her own beloved daughter lest anything should happen to her prematurely. So now brother Edward had turned his jealousy on this fine son of his.

'But even if he has a son I'm still the first born royal!' Aethelstan continued. 'I'm the next lawful king!' he insisted.

'Yes, you are indeed, so I'm going to have

2

the pleasure of your company while I train you!'

He brightened up a little, then with the honesty of his age blurted out, 'I don't like my father!'

'That certainly makes two of us,' she told herself. 'I must train him thoroughly in all tactical matters and supervise his weapons training as well. Life is going to be hard for him, through no fault of his own."

With great determination she concentrated upon a young boy's education. She noted he gave promise of being a natural warrior and there were times even when he could use his small sword with either hand—a most valuable asset in battle.

She took him around with her as she travelled from her favourite place of Tamworth.

'A wise king does not stop in one place,' she explained carefully. 'He always rides around his kingdom, often turning up unexpectedly, though when with a large court a courier has to go in advance to the reeve in charge of the next region. Men have to be fed and bedded in reasonable comfort. The idea of wandering is to keep men on their toes in case they get foolish ideas about conducting their personal feuds or revolts!'

He turned this over in his bright mind. 'It also keeps an enemy guessing, Aunt?'

'Very good, Aethelstan. Now we are nearing

3

the royal Saxon palace of Pucklechurch. It's not in a very good state of repair, I'm afraid. New timbers are needed in many places, but look!' She pointed forward on a higher part of land before them, which dropped away sharply. Their horses stood quietly, tired from a long mile-eating ride.

'Do you see danger?' she asked him quietly.

Aethelstan studied the scene below very carefully and took his time to answer.

'That big river in the distance. The Danes could sail up that easily to attack anywhere they fancied in this region.' He looked over at her where she sat her horse proudly, if displaying fatigue. Her gesith, her bodyguard, also stared as they clustered in a protective half circle.

'Correct, and they do—which is why I have had to increase the defences of Gloucester. The place had fallen into a mess so I ordered all the defensive walls to be rebuilt again, and a fyrd, a militia of trained men, ready and waiting. I also encouraged this knowledge to spread and the Danes have been a bit wary about Gloucester since then. I also worked out the core plan of the main streets so fighters could move easily to defend any point.'

'And it has worked, Aunt?'

'Very much so, and I also arranged fortified burghs all over Mercia, with men trained to turn to arms at any time.'

He knew he would never forget a word

she said because he adored her. Much as he missed seeing his mother he was honest enough, even so young, to realise he was being given a most superb education, vital for any future king. His personal tutor stretched his intellectual mind while highly trained fighters taught him how to use all of the weapons, the favourite of which was the sword. From waking to sleeping he had no spare time, because his wonderful aunt had so organised nearly all of his life. He was able to wander for a short while by himself, straightening his legs naturally, and it was then he fell into the habit of deep thinking. Something he was to do for the remainder of his life. He called these periods his 'thinking time".

Another day, when out riding, she talked to him about their society and culture. He had a rough idea but she now spelled out hard facts.

'Always understand a man's wergild as it is the most important to him after that of his oath,' she began one morning.

'A man's oath is of more value than his wife, son, sword or horse. It equates with his life but it is also a two-way affair. When an oath is given to a superior lord then that lord, in his turn, has to help the oath-giver. If a fighting man he has to provide his weapons and horse as well as feed and lodge him. Naturally on the man's death these goods go back to the lord. That's called the heriot, it's a kind of death duty and is perfectly reasonable if you think

5

about it.'

He considered and nodded in agreement and waited with expectation for more information. He knew deep in his bones that although his personal tutor saw to his intellectual needs it was from this wonderful aunt that he collected the knowledge of life.

'The men in your gesith, your bodyguard, they've given their oath to you?' he asked for extra clarification.

Aethelflaeda grinned. 'To me and not your father, which riles him enormously!' And she chuckled. 'He thinks because he's the male he should come first but your grandfather knows I'm superior to him!'

'But who reigns after Grandfather?' he asked shrewdly.

Aethelflaeda paused. It was a loaded question because King Alfred, whom some were already calling Alfred the Great, was a sick man. Indeed when she looked back down the years he had never really been anything else. It was something to do with his abdomen and even the most skilled of the old healing women could do nothing to help. He had achieved marvels during his reign with education for all, new, sensible laws, shipbuilding as well as fighting the Danes, though he had never been successful against the great troublemaker Northumbria. She had a nasty feeling he might not live much longer and where indeed did that leave her let alone

Aethelstan? She planned for her own and only offspring, her daughter, to be her heir and the next Lady of Mercia. Her husband, for whom she'd had little feelings, had died years ago. It was a marriage arranged by King Alfred with the best of intentions but it had been a hopeless mismatch.

The men would not hesitate to follow her but brother Edward? She did not trust him at all but was, for once, at a loss as to what to do for the best when King Alfred did die. If only this wonderful young nephew was a bit older. She gritted her teeth, aware his eyes were fixed on her face.

'Just you remember all I tell you. Now when we ride around pay attention to where we go. Always study the land as if you wanted to hold a battle on it. How suitable is it for violent fighting? Is there water? Is there a safe way to retreat for refuge? Could you be encircled from the rear? Never cease studying your surroundings. Acute observation could save your life, the lives of your warriors and your position as well!'

Aethelstan nodded seriously and knew he must always remember. After all, look at the battles and victories against the Danes conducted by this aunt. No wonder they hated her and were terrified of her appearing. She was well known for riding into battle, at the head of her warriors, wielding her sword with lethal skill.

Another day the lesson was on a fresh subject. 'Every man has a wergild,' she started. 'It indicates his worth. In a blood feud his enemy would know exactly what money he would have to pay to satisfy the Hundred Court's dictates for the dead or injured man's family. Every man who holds a hundred hides of land can also run a Hundred's Court. If the king should be in the area then he also sits with the chosen jury and adjudicates. So a man's wergild is of vital importance. A king has the highest wergild of all of course ...'

'But what happens when the trouble involves two kings?' he interrupted.

Aethelflaeda was not annoyed but delighted he was using his brain. She suspected he had a very good one as well. 'The king with the greatest territory becomes the superior because he can whistle up the largest army!'

'So the value of the wergild is decided upon exactly what a man owns,' he persisted, determined to get it all straight in his head.

'Right first time!' she praised. 'Now a slave is a non-person, usually of less value than an ox so he has nothing and can never give an oath to anyone!'

'Can they ever become free?' he wanted to know next.

'It depends upon their master. Some good masters will permit them to keep any coins they may earn and if they save them they may, one day, be able to purchase their own

8

manumission, but it is a pretty rare occurrence. Once a slave, always a slave. Some slave masters breed slaves as a business. Some are captured in battle, some foolish ones fall into debt and have to sell themselves into slavery to redeem their debt. If they mate with any female and there is a child then the infant is another slave but belongs to the slave master.'

This was all new to him and he crinkled his nostrils with distaste. There was something abhorrent in human slaves putting them below the value of cattle but he had to accept it was their way of life. How lucky he was to have been born royal, even if illegitimate.

'As you know I have a very loyal gesith but a king should also have a witan. About four men should do, who have lived long and know about life. A king does not have to take their advice but it is a foolish one who ignores wisdom and experience,' was another of her wise lessons that he also stored away in his head. There was certainly a lot to learn to become a king, because 'I will!' he vowed to himself. His father's wife had produced an infant boy then died, and now talk was he was seeking another to take her place. It dawned upon him that kings' wives were nothing but brood mares for the crown and this too made him crinkle his nose with disgust when he was on a solitary walk.

Aunt and nephew spent many hours in the saddle as she toured Mercia, though where his

9

father was he neither knew nor cared. There had been talk he had gone up to Northumbria to fight Danes but it appeared nothing much had come of that either.

His aunt showed him her fortifications at Gloucester as they rode for Stafford and then on to Tamworth. The river was awe-inspiring and on the far side were other tribes all with their own kings.

'You must never cease patrolling your land,' she emphasised yet again, 'and ride with your eyes wide open to learn your territory too. It would not surprise me if one day there is not some huge battle to try and unite this island once and for all. Remember! The defender picks the battle site. Not far from our royal palace at Pucklechurch there was a battle where King Ceawlin fought the three British tribes. They should have won hands down with the huge army they were able to muster when they united, but they were too cocky, complacent and short-sighted. They thought they had picked a perfect battle site with flat land in front of them on which to build defences. The trouble was it was on high land without water! Ceawlin was bright. He kept his men well back and out of range and just taunted them for hours. They raced around shouting personal challenges, and when King Ceawlin calculated he had exhausted them— without any water—he simply rolled forward and slew them piecemeal. He held his reserves back but when he did release them they stormed forward. The British had no chance. They ended up bolting, but downhill. Ceawlin's men followed them. Curved in at the bottom, trapped the British, and it was pure slaughter. All because a bad battle site had been chosen!' she told him.

Aethelstan listened enthralled. He pictured the scene and murderous slaughter all because of complacency. If he ever had to pick a battle site he would know exactly what to look for and what to avoid.

He grew but he would never make a giant of a man. He was fair, extremely handsome and already carried himself with an air of confidence. At the odd times his father did see him the older man did not like this one bit. His whole attention was now on this new son who was legitimate, and if his third wife could copy, two sons united should be able to drive this bastard one from the royal scene for all time. Certainly Wessex, he knew, would prefer legitimacy, though Mercia might prove difficult. That was all because of his sister and the magic she had woven over herself, which now spread to include Aethelstan. It was all so grossly unfair, so he just had to live as long as possible, till his legitimate offspring could take his place.

When Aethelflaeda checked with his tutor she was delighted to learn Aethelstan was considered outstandingly bright. He obviously

11

threw back in a direct line to his grandfather, King Alfred. His weapons instructors were equally enthusiastic, especially with the sword, so she placed an order with her armourer for a special adult one. It would be pattern welded, which took extreme skill with hot metals but gave the best and strongest sword for any man.

Aethelflaeda consulted very carefully with the man who made their weapons. She swore him to total secrecy without explaining why, but she was so popular and admired an explanation was not expected, except that she did say to the man, 'My brother Edward is never to know.'

A very strong sword was made by twisting bands of iron together and reheating them constantly, then edging with hard steel to give greater flexibility. The steel that finally cooled was virtually unbreakable and it would be given a double edge, and finally the sword face was polished. The hilt was built up around the tang, which was a continuation of the blade. The guard or quillon was often a single block of bone as well as cloth, leather or even silver wire. The grip would be highly decorated with metal plates and the tang riveted over a plate at the top of the hilt. The scabbard was usually made of two thin pieces of leather covered with wood, and its mouth would be ornamental. It would normally be lined with wool as the natural grease stopped rust. It was not only a superb weapon for a king but also an object of great beauty. It took many hours of work but she paid generously then wrapped the completed sword and scabbard in a long animal skin and hunted around for whom she wanted.

Cerdic and Ceorl were two members of her gesith whom she had known for a long time. She trusted them implicitly and when they stood before her she grinned triumphantly. Both of them were now well into their late thirties. Cerdic was a very fine warrior while Ceorl had become a quite famous scribe. They were two men who would be perfect for the start of her nephew's witan when he did become King.

She spoke quietly but with passion. 'I have had this sword made especially for Aethelstan when he does become King. Under no circumstances is my brother Edward to know about it, let alone see it. Will you two please hide this somewhere until the appropriate day comes.'

Cerdic and Ceorl exchanged uneasy looks. They did not like to hear their Lady talk in this vein. After all she was Mercia. Did she suspect something that was beyond them? The very thought of her brother being King stuck in their throats as they both disliked him intensely. Then they nodded, took her long parcel and decided where to hide it, in a place only they would ever know.

Aethelflaeda had read their unspoken

thoughts. She did have an instinct that her days were numbered now that King Alfred had died. If she should follow him Edward would demand to be King even though she had stipulated her daughter was to take her position. The trouble was her daughter could be a bit naïve. She was very fond of her Uncle Edward and looked up to him with admiration. Aethelflaeda had grave reservations that warning her daughter to be on her guard might well be a waste of time. Her heart ached for her daughter's welfare but she knew there was nothing whatsoever she could do. At least she mused she had seen Aethelstan on the right path. How he had developed as well! He had grown and was virtually a man. Although he would never be big and muscled he was superbly fit and trained to a hair.

There was very little else she knew she could do and she could only hope her daughter would develop a little sense and wisdom and stop hanging on every word her brother said as if it was a pearl of wisdom.

TWO

Aethelstan sat by himself on a rotting log, though he knew his gesith surrounded him at a distance. He still found it necessary to wander off by himself and commune with his thoughts, and he certainly had plenty at the moment.

It had all started to go wrong when his beloved aunt died quite suddenly and unexpectedly. His father had ridden off with his aunt's daughter but returned alone. Immediately his father proclaimed himself King.

Aethelstan was thunderstruck. 'But where is my cousin?'

His father simply made an airy explanation that she had gone to spend the rest of her natural life in a nunnery.

'But that's not right. Aunty said she was to be the next Lady of Mercia on her death!'

'Rubbish!' his father had snorted. 'I'm the king now and I say what goes on and she can live as a nun!'

Aethelstan could not let this treachery slide past. 'You're not meant to do that!'

'Well, I've done it, puppy, and you can forget any ideas in that line yourself. My wife is pregnant and I know it will be a son!'

'And what about my mother Ecgwyne?' he had accused hotly. 'Not good enough for you now, Father, even though she gave you me and a sister!'

'Bastards the pair of you!'

'And whose fault is that? Yours!'

'She was too low born!'

'Then why get her pregnant?' he had shot back.

'Don't you bandy words with me, your

15

king! Pity your precious aunt didn't drill some manners into you when you lived with her! Any sons I have now will come well before you because they will be legitimate. Not by-blows! Got that?'

'Grandfather planned for me to be King.'

'Well, he's not here but I am!' and he had lashed out with one hand and sent Aethelstan flying on his seat. 'Any more trouble from you as well and I'll . . .'

'You'll what, Father? Have me killed? Is that it? If so I think I'll have a word with the churchman who is visiting us here. If anything untoward should suddenly happen to me the Church will know where to look and question!'

'Why you . . . !'

But this time Aethelstan had adroitly removed himself from the range of his father's hands. He had indeed related all to a visiting bishop who had listened thoughtfully and said, 'You have done the right thing to speak out, my lord. I will see your worries go in the appropriate direction, but it might just be prudent to be careful. Get yourself a small gesith. A personal bodyguard with you at all times of day—and night!'

He had done just that though it rankled, but it had given him an early chance to get to know Cerdic and Ceorl. He had picked them almost at random, except his aunt had always spoken highly of them. Men older than he was but splendid fellows because he became acutely

16

aware he was so very much alone now. He missed his aunt's wisdom almost like a pain. He had fumed with anger at his father's deceit and treachery but there had been nothing he could do except wait until it was his turn. His father had married wife number three and now had two legitimate sons, but they were much younger than Aethelstan. He was a man and immediately called himself King and vowed he would be crowned on the royal Saxon stone at Kingston, where all the kings had been crowned in the past.

Then had come the shock and magnificent surprise of being presented with the most incredible sword. Cerdic and Ceorl had explained how it had come into their possession and the long months they had kept it secret from everyone, especially his father. It now rested on his left hip and his heart was choked with emotion as he thought of his wonderful aunt.

Now he had other problems. His father was dead and so was his eldest legitimate son called Aelfweard, his half brother, which was totally unexpected and without apparent reason, though Aethelstan had his suspicions. He knew he was very popular in Mercia, though there was still a faction in Wessex who opposed his position. He had no proof, no evidence, but suspected that Aelfweard's young death was no accident. Certainly he had been forced to arrange a double funeral. This

17

left Edwine the younger son to make a claim for the crown plus whoever else there was in Wessex who objected to a Mercian king, especially a bastard.

He had much to think about but had organised his witan. The first two members were Cerdic and Ceorl and he had also picked Oswald and Egbert as they were all roughly of an age. It was reassuring to know he had wise heads to turn to when the need arose and he acknowledged how fortunate he had been in having so much education from the Lady of Mercia. His gesith was comprised of men who had served his father, King Edward, though from odd grumbles he had picked up none of them had been enthusiastic about their position. How different it had all been with the Lady of Mercia. Now it was all up to him as the king.

He had made his plans, but bringing them to fruition would be another matter. Northumbria was, as always, the biggest problem because of the Danes and their Dane law. He had pondered long and hard about the important city of York, which the Danes insisted on calling Yorvik. His father had fought them but to no avail. What about diplomacy and treaties? It was commonsense to him the country should be united under the name of England, not just a hodgepodge of various old tribal names. What was the best way to go about this though, to make one race—the English? He knew he could muster a good-sized army but his mind would continue to revolve around diplomacy. Grandfather Alfred had believed in this whenever possible, just as he went out of his way to forge continental alliances. King Alfred had done his best but had never been able to make one England. It was going to be up to him. He thought about his four charming sisters. Some were still young but his one true sister was nearly ready for marriage. What better way to make a territorial union than with matrimony? This was something he intended to discuss in depth with his witan.

There was a sudden flurry of activity and two of his gesith strode forward pushing a young man ahead. Their spears were at his back.

'Over here!' Cerdic shouted as he and Ceorl appeared suddenly.

'What's this then?' Aethelstan asked, still a bit bemused at this interruption to important, complicated thoughts.

They all eyed a lanky young man who was so bedraggled and dirty he looked as if he had been rolling on the ground. He was taller than the rest of them but skeletally thin, almost emaciated. His features were regular without being outstanding, and his face was set in a mask of fear.

Rannulf eyed the men around him and realised he was in a very dangerous situation.

The two men with the spears were obviously a part of an important person's gesith. The two older men had superior rank because the spearmen deferred to them. Then his eyes turned and rapidly took in the young, fair-haired, wonderfully good-looking man. He was dressed in brightly coloured tunic and a half cloak with superior half trousers, hose, and embroidered cross garters ending above the most expensive boots he had ever seen. He suddenly realised by incredible luck he had come across the person he'd been seeking. He turned and focused respectful attention upon him who was obviously the king.

Rannulf dropped to his knees and raised both hands in supplication. 'Sire, please help me.'

Aethelstan had been expecting something like this for the last few minutes. It was not unexpected for a poor, wandering man to turn to a superior for aid.

'Who are you? What exactly do you want? Explain yourself!' he barked rather sternly.

Rannulf knew that what he said might well change the course of his life and he flogged his wits into action to speak coherently without exaggeration.

'I was born and bred as a slave near York!' he began carefully.

Immediately Aethelstan went onto high alert and waited with enormous interest for what else was to come.

Rannulf continued, picking his words with care, accuracy and the whole truth. 'They told me my mother died not long after my birth and the slave master made the rest of the slaves rear me. When I was old and strong enough he put me to work looking after his horses. I realise now he was a decent slave master, though the work was very hard indeed. Apart from breeding and selling slaves, he also sold horses and, now and again, when men came to buy horses from him they would give me a coin or two. My master allowed me to keep these coins, though they were of course his property, as a slave has nothing. I saved these coins and when I did eventually have enough he allowed me to buy my manumission. So, sire, I am a free man!'

'Prove it!' snapped Cerdic harshly.

Rannulf pulled a filthy tunic top to one side and extracted a small rolled-up parchment from around his neck, held in place by a grubby piece of cord. He handed this to the king and with enormous interest Aethelstan opened and read it, his eyebrows shooting up. He gave a brief nod to both Cerdic and Ceorl, who then read rapidly. They handed it back to the king with their nods of agreement, who in turn gave the precious document back to the young man.

'So!' Aethelstan said slowly. 'You tell us the truth!' and he took in the young man's bedraggled appearance. 'You don't look like a

21

very skilled fighter!' was his comment.

Rannulf nodded unhappily. 'I never had much chance to practise, sire, but I know I could improve!' he added hopefully.

'Have you ever given your oath to anyone?' was Aethelstan's next important question.

Rannulf nodded. 'To Anlaf son of King Sihtric, but I wasn't happy about it because I didn't like the man! But there was no one else. King Sihtric wouldn't see me. So I left to wander and find another man who would take my oath and I heard the king had his court at Tamworth for the time being. I have walked and walked and walked to get here, sire, and I am so hungry, wet through, tired and cold, but I want a home,' he explained wistfully. 'Please help me, sire,' he reiterated.

Aethelstan had already made his decision, but he looked at his two men with eyebrows elevated in silent question. Cerdic and Ceorl both gave a brief nod of acceptance. New young blood, capable of being trained in something was always of value.

'Very well!' Aethelstan agreed. 'Swear your oath to me now before these two elders of my witan!'

Rannulf stood, bowed his head and made his vow to serve faithfully and loyally, then he looked hopefully at the king who was now his new master. A great relief filled him and he wondered if he could be forward and speak again.

22

'Sire, I could work with your horses as well as practise with weapons to become a foot soldier, but there is something much more important I would love to do. I want to learn how to read and write! I have looked and looked at writing and tried to understand how all these lines and signs make sounds for conversation. Please!' he begged openly.

Ceorl stiffened with great interest. This was his department as he was the king's royal scribe, but he was all alone. The thought of having a pupil to teach and bring on and do some of the work was most interesting. He had sound reason to believe that this king would turn into a dynamic one and there would be many charters as well as ordinary writing of letters and messages. An assistant trained by himself in his ways was most attractive. He caught the king's eye and gave a nod. The trouble was, could he learn? Did he have the necessary brains? He would be able to tell in few days.

Aethelstan was pleased. Ceorl would never be able to cope on his own with what he had in mind for England's expansion. Where would he live though? Cerdic and his wife Edith, who was his treasure and joy, had their only daughter Osburga due back at any time from the home where she had been undergoing domestic training. Ceorl lived alone. He looked at him with another silent question, which the scribe understood immediately and with which he certainly agreed.

'He can live with me, sire!'

'Good!' Aethelstan approved, which sorted out one problem. 'I take it you have no wergild?'

Rannulf shook his head miserably. A man going around without any wergild was almost as disgusting as going without his small clothes.

Aethelstan now considered very carefully, as rank was of critical importance. Directly above a slave was the gebur, who paid his dues to his lord in money or produce and worked on his lord's land, to the bailiff or reeve's directions. Above him was a cottar who paid no rent but who, throughout the year, worked for his lord in return for having five acres of land, on which to keep a cow and grow his own food. Above this rank was the geneat who also paid rent and carried out many duties for the reeve or bailiff belonging to the lord. Sometimes they were also regarded as companions. The best class of all though was that of the churl. They made the backbone of the country and if they fancied wandering somewhere they were perfectly free to do this. They could own and inherit land and pay their dues direct to the Crown and Church, and also took part in the folkmoot and military service. It was an excellent rank. Directly above all these were the very important earldormen, and it was Aethelstan's intention to make the four members of his witan into this rank, with a

24

hundred hides of land each.

'I am going to make you a churl!' he
flatly and Rannulf went pink with deli
This was something he had never expected in
his wildest dreams. From slave to churl! The
whole world was wide open to him and he
vowed to become one of the best scribes ever
and serve this king with his life. 'Now I think
you had better take him away, Ceorl, clean
him up, feed him, give him a good night's rest,
then start to make him into a scribe!' and he
smiled with the very considerable charm and
manners for which he was renowned.

Ceorl started the very next day once
Rannulf was cleaned up and in fresh clothes
provided by Cerdic.

'There are two alphabets, runic and ogham,
but I don't bother with the latter as it's far too
slow. Here is the runic alphabet. Get it in your
head then we'll take it from there. It's up to
you but I expect results otherwise you'll get my
stick across your back!' he warned and was not
joking. An assistant scribe would be a Godsend
but was this unusual young man capable? He
was reassured within two days and secretly
amazed. Rannulf had grasped the alphabet
and even started to string tiny words together.
With immense pleasure Ceorl threw himself
into tutoring, making plans, at the same time,
to ease a workload he knew was going to come
any day from this dynamic king.

'I'm amazed with him!' he confided in

Cerdic. 'I wouldn't have thought it possible for someone so green and uneducated to grasp runic writing as he has done!'

'A natural?' Cerdic suggested.

'Very much so. Tell the king when you have time!'

*   *   *

Edwine was a deeply worried young man, and now had more than a little fear. It had taken some time to work it out but he considered the problem had been solved at last. It was quite shocking to accept his father King Edward and his older brother Aelfweard had both died so suddenly, within days of each other. The upstart, the bastard King Aethelstan, had held a double funeral.

He was the next legitimate son in the royal line to be the proper king, but he was realist enough to know he was far too young and without enough men to challenge Aethelstan. His brother had been a fine, fit and healthy person, so how had he died and so rapidly? His mind went back to their last meal together. His brother had always adored cooked mushrooms with a stew, and what was easier than slipping in some poisonous toadstools for him to eat? He had personally disliked mushrooms and had eaten poultry instead, while his brother had tucked in with gusto, even having more than one helping. He knew it would be a useless task to interrogate the cooks, which meant he, the sole male survivor, might now also be in danger. It was a very frightening thought to one so young. The sensible thing to do would be to flee somewhere until he was bigger, older and could command more men with confidence. Somewhere over the sea, but which way, east or west?

West, he told himself, to Dublin, but he dare not go alone. He must have an escort, and then he remembered he had seen two footloose churls around. Money! He must have some to pay them to escort him and arrange a sea crossing. He knew where money was kept that had been his dead brother's, and without pausing to think it through any further he went into what had been his brother's chamber. He rummaged around and with relief found some coins. Were they enough? He could only hope so. Wandering churls were usually short of cash and were happy enough to do anything to earn some.

He went outside and bumped into them straightaway. When he beckoned they trotted over. One was middle-aged and the other much younger.

'Your names?' he asked.

The older one spoke for both of them. 'I am called Aidan and my son here is called Edred, Lord.'

It was on the tip of his tongue to correct them, then he realised it would be foolish to expect them to call him sire when he was obviously not. A fresh wave of fury at Aethelstan filled him for a moment but he hastily pushed this away to concentrate on more immediate matters.

'I wish to go over to Dublin and I need an escort to take me to the coast and to arrange passage on a suitable vessel. I will pay this!' and he showed his coins.

Aidan examined them, did a rapid calculation and nodded for both of them. 'When would you wish to start, Lord?'

'As soon as possible, and get there quickly. Can you do this for me?'

Aidan nodded. 'Yes, Lord. If you can be ready first thing in the morning I will have three good horses and we could set off straightaway!'

'Excellent!' and with relief at having solved a major problem Edwine went to consider what he should take with him. The minimum clothes were needed—he would always be able to get replacements in Dublin. All he wanted to do was get away, grow big and strong then come back at the head of his own army and crush Aethelstan once and for all.

Just under a week later he was amazed at the sight of the sea. It did not seem possible there could be so much water going on and on into the horizon, and not far away over there would be the refuge of Dublin. They showed him a little boat for which they had negotiated and he was dubious at first. It seemed a very small craft to go out over this mighty sea and they sensed his doubts.

'You would not want anything bigger, Lord, because you would have more crew and people would know and it would cost you more money. This little craft is perfectly seaworthy and is crewed by two people only. One to handle the sail, the other to steer. You will be in Dublin in no time at all. I would suggest you come aboard and we will get you a hot meal and the crew will come and tie up alongside in a little rowing boat.'

Still a little bit uneasy, Edwine finally agreed and did as had been suggested. He was also conscious that the coins he had paid had been limited. He simply could not afford a larger ship and neither did he dare to tarry in the place where his father and brother had died. His instinct warned him his life was imperilled—he could be safe only in Dublin.

The cabin was very small but had a comfortable bunk on one side. The two churls gave him a nutritious hot broth and he soon felt sleepy. He woke once at some time in the night, and the little craft was bobbing along happily over the sea, just meeting one or two white horses. The man at the tiller was old and grizzled, the other, who handled the sail, was young and athletic. Quite satisfied and still feeling sleepy he returned to the cabin.

When he did awaken the second time and

climbed the couple of steps from the cabin, he was shocked to see it was full daylight and he was quite alone. He stumbled around on legs not at all used to the motion of a boat and saw the little rowing boat had also vanished. There was no one in the craft but himself, and when he looked up the sky had turned ugly and threatening. The white horses on the sea were now more prolific and the little craft had started to bounce from bow to stern, then sway from one side to the other. His stomach groaned, gave an almighty heave and he was heartily sick over the side. Not knowing anything about the sea, he had picked the wrong side and his vomit blew back on him.

Now fear filled him. He had not the faintest idea what to do to sail a craft and the one sail was quite beyond him. The little craft now began to swing to both sides and the sea started to ship over the gunwales. It was at this point he realised he was going to die like his brother. This had all been very cleverly planned. He looked round in a panic when all to be seen was ocean, very white-capped waves getting larger and more turbulent as the sky became blacker.

Then it happened quite suddenly. The little craft went to port and the sea gushed in with force, so that within seconds she had begun to sink. Edwine was flung into the water and frantically tried swimming strokes, but the water was icy cold and, when he gasped, it

30

flooded his mouth. He opened it to let out a wail of terror and distress and the sea poured into his mouth, rushed into his lungs and he died knowing that he too had been murdered.

*   *   *

Cerdic was slightly on edge, calculating the days and waiting, not saying a word to his pal Ceorl on the rare time they had together when the scribe was not busy tutoring his pupil.

When the day came it was in the afternoon as they both appeared and asked for Lord Cerdic. He strode over to them very quickly, eyes flashing a silent question.

Aidan again spoke for both of them. 'It is done, Lord. We waited until the body was washed ashore!'

'Very good work!' Cerdic praised and went to his private saddlebag, inside which was a purse heavy with coins. He selected two, not large but of gold, then returned and handed one to each man. 'What are your plans now?'

Aidan was delighted with this payment, far more than he had expected. 'We thought we would ride around a bit again because we always know where to find the king's court.'

Cerdic gave a grim smile. 'Always make sure it is me!' he warned them soberly. 'Good reliable men are needed at all times and if you should hear any more useful information, come to me and you'll be suitably rewarded

31

again!' he promised.

Cerdic hastily spoke to Ceorl then went to seek out his king. When found he planted himself face to face and switched a bland expression in his eyes. 'News just in, sire,' he opened.

Aethelstan went on the alert. He was not in the least fooled by Cerdic, who was also rather tensed up. 'Yes?' he asked in his usual polite manner.

'It's just reached my ears through two wandering churls that your half-brother Edwine has drowned at sea.'

'What!' and Aethelstan was staggered, totally unprepared for this. 'At sea?'

'Yes, sire. It appears he was going to Dublin but something went wrong and a storm came up. The boat foundered and Edwine simply drowned. An accident. His body was washed ashore and . . .' Cerdic waved two hands expressively.

Aethelstan took a deep breath and looked over at a tree. He knew he didn't believe a word of this accident. It simply did not ring true, yet he knew he could neither say nor do anything. Edwine would have grown into violent opposition so his loyal men had simply arranged to remove this problem as he suspected they had removed the elder brother. His heart went out to them and he continued to stand and say nothing. Did he feel sorrow? No, he admitted to himself. It was just another obstacle removed, albeit a harsh action, but he realised he was lucky to have such devoted followers.

'I see,' he managed to get out with equal blandness. Now was the time to change the subject. 'As you and your fellow members of the witan have become eorldormen, I am going to arrange with the scribe for you all to become hundred-hides men. This means of course as you will be travelling around with my royal court it is important that the four of you choose very good reeves to look after your property and rents while you are absent. I don't suppose every reeve is totally honest. It will be human nature for them to dip into your rents now and again, but that becomes your problem!' he said with a smile. 'At the same time I realise you will all wish to build homes more appropriate to your status. I don't have to remind you that in these modern times we are still often at the mercy of gangs of Danes who are out to get what they can. You'll need good sentries, tall, solid palisades and perhaps even a small fighting force to defend your homes when away with me.'

Cerdic nodded thoughtfully. 'Yes, sire, you are very right indeed. What are your plans, sire?'

Aethelstan considered for a moment. 'I wish to get my eldest half sister married to Sihtric of York. He is a pagan so he'll have to turn to be a Christian. I want an invitation to go to him

33

to come down to my royal court at Tamworth, and he can be married there to my sister Eadgyth. She is old enough to get married, and like the rest of my sisters she has turned into a very beautiful lady. Sihtric must then accept me as Over King for the whole of this country. It is absolutely ridiculous this island be split up into segments when, if it was united, it would be quite powerful.'

Cerdic thought about this a moment. 'But what about Dane law, sire?'

Aethelstan nodded wisely. 'That will have to be broken eventually. I realise I will have to take this a step at a time, but not only will this island be England, the language will be English, the currency, the laws—while everything to do with Dane law will have to vanish. In due course I shall issue my own charters, but first of all I must have York, which will leave me the whole of Northumbria. I am hoping that marriage and diplomacy will prevail. If it does not though, I go to war—but a united England I will have. It was what my grandfather King Alfred the Great wanted so desperately and he tried so hard, but it was not meant to be. My father King Edward also wanted to take Northumbria, but to no avail. So did my wonderful aunt the Lady of Mercia, but I realise now she was ahead of her time. It is all going to be up to me.'

Later on he related this conversation to Ceorl and, after him, the other witan members,

Oswald and Egbert.

Ceorl was the most thoughtful when receiving this information. 'It's a good job I have an assistant now because there's going to be an awful lot of writing coming up, I can see.'

'How is your pupil managing?'

Ceorl shook his head with amazement. 'I would not have thought it possible anyone could grasp so quickly the alphabet and the construction of small words. He has even begun on sentences and his grammar is decent! He is a very pleasant young man to have in the home. Indeed, between the two of us, I am thinking of adopting him. To date, I could not hope to have had a better son!'

Cerdic was quite amazed. 'That's a big step!' he said carefully. 'I hope you have thought long and hard on this. We know nothing about his background. He doesn't himself!'

'That's true, but there is something quite fine in him. He thinks he is about eighteen years. How old is your daughter?'

'Steady! Osburga will soon be fifteen years and she'll be home any day, but she's very spirited and has a will of her own, so don't you get ideas in your head about matchmaking!'

Ceorl grinned at him and strolled off. Later on that evening Cerdic related everything to his beloved wife Edith.

'Osburga is home tomorrow,' she confirmed, 'but as for what she would think to a strange young man, your guess is as good as mine. A number of fine young fellows have been paraded before her and she has turned up her nose at all of them. Now what's this you are saying about a new home?'

'The king is right. We are now people of status and must live accordingly, so I'm going to get some plans drawn up, prepare to hire some slaves with a good bailiff, and all being well we will have a large fine home before winter sets in. We both like this area of Mercia, so it can be here.'

'Will this hundred hides of land be folk land in writing, or folk land by custom?' she asked in a practical voice.

'It is going to be in writing, capable of inheritance to our heir, so extremely valuable. Ceorl is going to be very busy indeed, and without his new assistant he might have had problems.'

'I find it amazing to think we are now people of worth and such status. This means Osburga becomes a good catch for any young man!' she pointed out shrewdly.

Cerdic had already thought of that but there were very few young men around. Only Rannulf, and did he really want a husband for his daughter who was slave born and bred? This was a difficult question and he shied away from a direct answer.

Edith adored her husband and could read him so easily. 'Handsome is as handsome does!' she said a little tartly. 'Ceorl is nobody's fool. If he feels he wants to adopt a son then good luck to him. He must get very lonely at times.'

Ceorl did and he almost envied the marital and domestic bliss of his friend. He eyed Rannulf carefully as he studiously bent to perfect his writing. It was so satisfying understanding how these signs made conversation when he had puzzled and pondered with frustration all through those previous unhappy years.

'Goodness knows when I'll ever be as fast as you, sir,' he said to Ceorl with a shake of his head.

Ceorl grinned. 'I'll tell you my secret. I have memorised my own private signs for many common words like "and", "but" and "the", for example. A kind of shortened writing version when speed is of the essence, but to do a document properly everything must be written out in detail as I've shown you.'

Rannulf was amazed. 'What a splendid idea, sir. I'll give it some thought. I did wonder how you could be so fast!' Then he halted, curious but not wishing to be thought rude. He had never dreamed he would ever be so well fed, dressed and comfortable. It turned his slavery days back to a nightmare.

'Curious over something?' Ceorl guessed.

Rannulf went scarlet then gave a little nod. 'No wife?' he had to ask.

37

Ceorl paused and puckered his lips. The question was understandable from someone sharing his small home. Edith, Cerdic's wife, cooked for him so he ate well and was much happier now he had the company of this young man, for whom he was developing a healthy respect. His intellectual capabilities were proving quite astounding and he accepted he had found a most worthy successor. Just a little more polish was needed and young Rannulf would be able to write a document to match his work. He was a valuable asset to Mercia.

'I am divorced. I married when I was far too young and green. I saw a pretty face, was bewitched and plunged into matrimony. It lasted about five years, then she divorced me because she said I spent too long away from home on my job. It was just an excuse of course because we were quite mismatched. Under our sensible laws she was entitled to and took half of all I owned, which left me rather poverty stricken. Without my scribe's work it would all have been bleak indeed. That's all years ago now. What happened to her I neither know nor care,' and he halted again as he went back down the years, giving his companion a rueful look.

'During that ghastly period I did see someone I thought quite remarkable. It was for exactly five days only. She had lovely blonde hair but her most outstanding attraction was the bluest eyes I have ever seen.

Her name was Judith but I was in such a state from the divorce and all the uproar in general I did not even manage to speak to her. Then when I plucked up courage she had gone. Vanished seemingly into thin air. Who she was and from where she came I never knew. Also I have never stopped looking for her but to no avail. For all I know she may be dead or married with many children, but I will never forget her. She was so lively and vivacious my heart went out to her. It was all my fault for not speaking, or at least finding out from where she came. So if you ever find a young woman who attracts you do not hurry into a relationship. Take it slowly to be certain but on the other hand speak your mind so she knows your interest!' he advised sincerely.

Rannulf knew these were words of wisdom, and the next morning they hammered back at him when he first saw Osburga. She was with her mother Edith and they were the young and old version of the same. He gave a polite smile and nod to both of them, then went about his business thinking at the speed of a galloping horse. She was the only young person around them but was he in any position to try and strike up a friendship?

Ceorl understood in a flash and he just hoped his words of wisdom had lodged in Rannulf's mind. He was not sure whether he liked Osburga or not. She was very spirited and could be argumentative, and he suspected both Edith and Cerdic had their hands full with her temperament.

Rannulf had not gone unnoticed either. 'Who is he?' Osburga asked her mother, so Edith explained in detail.

'Slave born and bred?' Osburga repeated and her lips curled a little with distaste.

Edith did not miss this. 'Don't turn your nose up at him,' she rebuked. 'He is a rather fine young man and very talented indeed. What's more I predict he is going places. Whether he would wish to get to know you is another matter. Let's face it, daughter, you are inclined to be choosy and if you don't watch it you might end up being left behind!'

Osburga flinched a little because it was unusual for her mother to speak so caustically. They were very fond of each other and she adored her father as well as respected him. It was just then she saw the king striding down and she bowed her head respectfully, as did Edith.

Aethelstan had a lot on his mind, most of which concerned York and Northumbria in general. He saw Cerdic and beckoned for him to come over and spoke so everyone could hear.

'I want a messenger to go up to Sihtric and invite him and his court down to my court at Tamworth, where he can marry my sister. He has to become a Christian first though, so I need a good bishop present. A proper Church bishop too, not the fighting variety!' he said firmly.

Some of the bishops went around with their own mercenaries and were perfectly capable of dealing with local Church matters as well as resorting to loot. Aethelstan was inclined to look down his nose at such people but the proper Church bishops did not wander far and could be thin on the ground. As far as he was concerned, any bishop would do to instruct Sihtric to become a Christian and marry his eldest sister. Once this was done he knew there were other matters to deal with. He was perfectly well aware a faction still existed in Wessex who objected strongly to him being King. It had even reached the ears of the witan they wanted to attack and blind him. It was vital therefore he send a small army down into Wessex to subdue opposition once and for all. When would he ever be able to get himself crowned at Kingston upon Thames? It looked difficult, though he would have to go to make his position positive with the archbishop. In many ways Grandfather Alfred, though constantly battling the Danes, had not been in a position where so many people wished to kill him. He had been such a popular and respected king. There was also the matter of arranging for ships to be built, which would take considerable time. He knew in his bones and instinct that a fleet would be necessary some time in the future to sail north, even if he did get Northumbria to submit and accept him as the overall king.

There were the Scots to deal with. There were also Welsh kings. It seemed nobody had the wisdom to realise unification of the country was the answer to all future problems and enemies. His other sisters must be married to royals on the continent for alliances over there. Grandfather Alfred had started this but never progressed far enough for sufficient help to join him to sweep the Danes away completely. Aethelstan could only hope that this was the right time. He blessed the fact he had so many charming half sisters. He had only one half brother, who was still far too young and small to get ideas in his head. Edmund perhaps, when he became a man, would be an ally not an enemy. He intended to see as much of Edmund as possible to influence him. Although he was a great believer in diplomacy and the bonds of matrimony, he had a suspicion, deep in his guts, that one day there would be the most mighty battle. Where and when this would take place he had not the faintest idea, but he knew his instinct was correct. He had instructed the men of his witan to keep his soldiers fully trained and fit at all times. How they performed in battle would one day be crucial to him. He gave a deep sigh and walked away, his mind busy.

'He is carrying the cares of the world on

his shoulders,' Cerdic nodded thoughtfully. 'I would not want to wear a crown for all the gold in the world!'

THREE

Aethelstan gave a huge sigh of relief as Sihtric's large party started on their way back to York. It had been a very difficult time from the moment he had arrived as an avowed pagan. The thought of having to take instruction to become a Christian had not greatly pleased him but one sight of a beautiful girl had changed his mind. In Aethelstan's opinion he did not look a very healthy specimen of manhood and he was certainly so much older than his bride or even Aethelstan.

When the party had finally disappeared Aethelstan called Ceorl to him for a private conversation. 'I have very important work for you to do, which is no concern or to be privy to anyone else until I state. I will eventually inform my witan but you must do the work first. I will never marry and reproduce.'

Ceorl was staggered at this statement and had no words but simply looked inquiringly at his king.

Aethelstan began to explain. 'There has been so much trouble over me becoming King that I want my will to be drawn up stating that after me comes my half brother Edmund. As soon as we get to our home territory this is to be given priority!' he said firmly.

Ceorl could only nod, still rather taken aback by the statement. 'Who will have custody of this will and witness it, sire?'

'It is my wish that the bishop rides back with us, witnesses and takes the will to lodge in the safekeeping of the Church. Perhaps that would stop all arguments if anything should happen to me prematurely. I still have not been crowned King on the royal Saxon stone. There has been no time, what with one thing and another, so that is something else for you to organise. I have to deal with Wessex. I intend to ride down there, crack a few skulls, break a few bones and perhaps Wessex will eventually get the message that I and I alone am the king of England.'

Ceorl nodded. This private conversation certainly made sense but he could see he had a lot of work coming up and obviously Rannulf was not to be involved. It was *too* private.

'I will inform my witan only when the will has been executed and is in the custody of the Church. Perhaps then I might have a bit of peace and quiet to go about a king's business!' and the king smiled.

He had great respect and liking for this insignificant little man who was so brilliant at what he did. He admired Cerdic and even the other two members of his witan, and realised he was quite fortunate in that respect.

Ceorl hesitated only a moment then turned to his king. 'I have a bit of a problem, sire, and would be grateful for your advice,' he started.

Aethelstan stiffened with interest. He could not remember when last Ceorl had asked for something, and he knew if it was in his power to grant it he would do so.

'What is it?' he asked gently. This was the other side of giving an oath. The oath-taker had the obligation of helping the giver when possible.

'As you know, sire, I am a divorced man and although Cerdic and Edith are kind enough to give me the run of their home, when I go back inside my four walls it can be very lonely. Not any more though. I have young Rannulf, who really is the most excellent company, and I predict something—he is going places. I'm impressed with what he has learned and his skill to date. It is quite possible he will leave me behind one day as he matures and acquires more skill and knowledge. I have been thinking of adopting him as my son. I know he was slave born and bred but somewhere in him there is some unusually good blood. What do you think of this idea, sire?'

Aethelstan did not hesitate. He had formed a very good opinion of the young ex-slave. Often he never passed comment about a person, but neither did he miss anything. 'I think this is a splendid idea and I will be quite prepared to be his sponsor!'

'Oh, sire, would you?' Ceorl gasped not quite expecting this honour.

'Yes! But get my work done first if you don't mind!' he said kindly but firmly.

Cerdic had not seen the two of them in such a long conversation, nor the various expressions that had crossed his friend's craggy features. He had not the faintest idea what this could involve, and he had no intention of asking. When the time was right Ceorl would confide in him and he was quite happy to wait. His friend looked so blissfully happy at this moment that it had to be something quite magnificent. Puzzle his brains as he might, he could not think what on earth it might be.

'Now let's ride on and get back to our home territory. We will rest for two nights, then I'm going skull-breaking in Wessex and before I am much older I am going to Kingston to get myself crowned once and for all. A king without a crowning is not much of a king.'

Rannulf watched with interest as Ceorl took a fine, thin sheet of writing leather and started to mix his inks. Soon he intended to get expensive parchment for important documents, but had none at present. Thin skins, well tanned, were very good but parchment was more modern and he did not believe in being behind the times.

Ceorl looked up at him from where he sat at his table. 'Clear off this time. It's something

46

private for the king and bishop. Go and take a walk!' he ordered.

Rannulf obeyed but with mind buzzing. He stood a little aimlessly wondering where to go, then spotted the young daughter of Edith and Cerdic, who had just returned. She was no beauty but carried herself well with a frank, open look. She wore dark brown half trousers with a tunic to match and a long cloak. Osburga stared back at him and they both said 'Hello!' at the same time and grinned.

'I'm Rannulf!' he introduced himself.

'Osburga—and you were born and bred a slave I hear?'

Rannulf thought he could hear a disparaging note in her voice and knew he flushed. 'That's hardly my fault, girl, is it?' he shot back at her, planting his feet firmly apart and stared hard with a degree of coldness.

Osburga was startled as she sensed hostility. Just who did he think he was? Another upstart, cocky male. What was this about a slave becoming a scribe? Uncle Ceorl must have gone mad.

She gave a sniff, which spoke volumes, and walked on. Edith joined him. 'Don't take on,' she asked quietly. 'She can be a handful but you two are the only youngsters here at present and she's only just returned home. She'll come round, give her time,' she told him gently.

Rannulf liked Edith. She was so homely,

47

full of good sense and adored her Cerdic. He pulled a face then managed a wan smile. How wonderful it must be to have a parent, a personal family. So later on that evening, when they were alone, Ceorl spoke to him.

'I am willing to adopt you as my son. Interested?'

Rannulf was shocked. Then he gave a wide smile. 'There's nothing I'd like better, sir. Do you really mean it? What do I have to do?'

Ceorl chuckled at his enthusiasm. 'You do nothing specific,' he explained. 'The king is going to sponsor you and there will be a small ceremony before the witan, then everyone else!'

Rannulf bowed his head, swallowed hard and felt a prickle at the back of his eyes. 'It doesn't seem possible!' he murmured emotionally. 'A real father. A proper home. A family!'

Ceorl saw he must lighten the atmosphere. 'A family of just two!'

Rannulf stared back at him unable to halt two tears of happiness. 'What can I say?'

'Nothing, son. Just be yourself and carry on as before. Now I must see the king again before he retires for the night!' and taking the document on which he had laboured all day he went to the tent the king used when travelling.

Rannulf stepped outside too and looked up at the sky. There would be a full moon this evening, and the stars overhead were silver

48

jewels.

'Out late?' Osburga said appearing unexpectedly.

Rannulf nearly jumped with shock and turned to eye her. 'So?' he made himself drawl.

Now it was Osburga's turn to flush. 'I'm sorry. I was rude earlier. Forgive me?' she asked humbly but with sincerity.

He gave her a beaming smile, leaned forward and bestowed a gentle kiss on her soft lips. 'Of course!' Then he knew he simply must tell someone. 'I'm going to be adopted. I'm going to become part of a family, albeit a small one and the king will sponsor me!'

Osburga could not have been more surprised or impressed. 'He will? You are! That's magnificent for you,' and her voice rang with sincerity. 'Come to my home and tell my parents!' and she grabbed his arm and dragged him forward, burst in and told the news.

Cerdic smiled. It must be all right if the king was to stand sponsor. Edith beamed with her own delight. She had formed a favourable impression of this young man and had been furious with her daughter's caustic comments and made this plain too.

'This calls for your best brewed ale, my joy!' Cerdic pronounced, and Edith hurried off. They had all just settled with their drinks when there was a figure at the door, behind which was Ceorl. They all stood respectfully as the king strode forward. He faced Edith. 'May I,

49

good wife?' he asked with his usual, exquisite manners.

They bustled around to find extra stools and full mugs, then the king lifted his drink and raised his hand to salute Rannulf.

'Tomorrow, first thing, I ride to Wessex!' Aethelstan explained. 'The bishop will depart in the morning, also under escort of course.' He looked at each of them in turn. The calibre of these people made the backbone of England, even though all four members of his witan had started to slow down and usually fell out of the saddle instead of dismounting with their stiff, ageing knees. Now was the time to explain. It could be common knowledge from tomorrow. 'I've just drawn up my will with the bishop as witness. I will never marry myself because of all the uproar there's been. The next king will be my half brother Edmund, who should hopefully have reached manhood by then.'

Cerdic was not in the least surprised. The others were, but upon reflection acknowledged the wisdom of the action. They nodded and Aethelstan was pleased. Trust these sensible down-to-earth people to understand in a flash.

The king continued. 'When I return from breaking skulls in Wessex I'm riding to get myself crowned. All can come who wish to,' he invited and smiled at his audience, all of whom nodded their heads enthusiastically. A crowning was a very rare event indeed.

'But before I go anywhere, this young man,' and he nodded at Rannulf, 'will acquire his dad!'

Which was exactly what happened. It was a short ceremony before the witan, then Ceorl drank more ale with everyone else. 'Don't ask for any scribe's work today, sire,' he warned with a hiccup.

Aethelstan laughed. 'I'm not so sure I'll be riding far today either,' he admitted. 'But a start must be made. To horse, men!' he shouted to his gesith, and there was a wild scramble to tighten girths and mount up. With a flurry from their hooves the war party trotted away.

'I think I feel sorry for those fools in Wessex,' Cerdic murmured thoughtfully to no one in particular, then he stiffened with surprise as two men appeared escorted by the outer-fringe sentries.

Cerdic walked forward and beckoned the men aside, where they could converse privately. He eyed them with a frown. He smelled trouble.

'Was not expecting you back so soon,' he said sharply, and waited for Aidan to speak, with Edred standing alongside.

Aidan began to speak rapidly with Edred giving the odd nod of confirmation. Cerdic frowned at what he heard then gritted his teeth.

'You are sure of your facts?' he questioned

sternly, though he had not found this pair in the past indulging in exaggeration. 'Go over it all again. I want every detail of your observations and knowledge. Some may seem unimportant to you but not to me, so think carefully.'

The two wandering churls looked at each other then took it in turns to speak, with an identical story and comments. When they had finished Cerdic went into his home and dived into his neck purse for money. Edith lifted her eyebrows in silent question.

'Feed and give them beds while they are here, will you, my joy,' he asked her. 'They bring important information as always. Wandering churls really are the best news carriers,' he explained.

Edith was curious but knew when not to question and hurried away to check she had enough stew in her cauldron. Cerdic went back to the churls and paid them generously.

'My wife will see to your needs. I expect you are pretty hungry for a proper meal.'

'We are, Lord,' Aidan confirmed. 'We've stayed overnight at some places and the food was lousy,' he grumbled.

Cerdic wasn't interested in that. 'I take it you'll be wandering again?'

Aidan shook his head for both of them. 'We're getting fed up with it, especially when winter comes. Could we give our oaths to the king?'

Cerdic had sensed this was coming. Two fighting men were always an asset. 'Where are your families?'

'My wife died of disease,' Aidan explained with a heavy voice.

'And mine died after giving birth to twins. They all died,' Edred explained. 'And it'll be a long time before I put myself through that experience again!' he said bitterly. 'I prefer to stay single and when I want a female take a slave!'

'Not here you won't!' Cerdic barked. 'We look after our slaves, which is why they work so well and willingly. The first person that bothers my slaves will die quickly, and don't underestimate my age either!' he warned with a degree of savagery in his voice.

The two churls eyed each other. They believed him. If they wished to keep breathing they left this lord's slaves very much alone.

'I am an earldorman and a hundred-hide man!' Cerdic told them, and they nodded as they received this second warning. This was a very important person; better on their side than against them. This man's wergild was enormously high. Very politely and respectfully they bowed their heads in acquiescence.

Cerdic knew he had made the necessary point. 'I'll speak to the king when he returns,' and he smothered a smile. 'I don't think he'll be away that long!'

Then Edith appeared and beckoned them inside. 'Wash first and change into these clean clothes. Out the back, at once if you wish to eat,' she ordered. 'You both stink!'

Even Cerdic was surprised at the king's return after only a week. 'That was quick, sire!'

Aethelstan grinned at his favourite witan member. He vaulted from his saddle, stretched his arms and slapped Cerdic on his shoulders with delight. 'Now perhaps I can go to Kingston and get myself crowned! I have never heard of a king having to wait quite so long to get the crown on his head!'

Cerdic pulled a face and gave a tiny shake of his head. 'News came in while you were away, sire!'

Aethelstan knew his man so well and he did not like the serious look on Cerdic's face. He took a deep breath and shook his head. 'Don't tell me there is someone else?'

'I'm afraid so, sire. His name is Elfred and from going back over your royal family tree I think he must be the grandson of the king who reigned for that short time, before Great King Alfred!'

Aethelstan put his mind to the latest problem. 'I suppose that makes us some kind of cousins?'

'Yes, sire! And it appears he says his claim to the throne is stronger than yours, because his grandfather was King before yours!'

Aethelstan winced visibly. Another

problem! Another potential usurper. Another delay to his crowning.

Cerdic read him easily. He related the conversation he had had with the wandering churls, not missing a word or an idea. 'From what these two have said this Elfred is not the most healthy specimen. He has some kind of breathing problem and is often short of breath. What you want me to do, sire?'

Aethelstan did not hesitate. 'No more outright killing. I cannot allow myself to go and be crowned leaving a trail of corpses behind me. I think the best way to handle this is for him to be frightened out of this country so that he bolts for Normandy, and with a bit of luck he'll become ill there and die naturally. What do you think?'

'Perfect, sire, and quite easy to arrange. Also there is another matter. These two churls have become fed up with wandering, and they wished to give their oaths to you. The older one, the father, is all right but Edred the younger one may have to be watched.' He explained why. 'I look after my oxen perfectly as I do my slaves. That is why they work so well for me. They trust me and I have it in mind to manumit a couple of them, a female in the house to help Edith and one outside to supervise the building of my new home, and of course Ceorl's.'

'Very sensible!' Aethelstan replied. 'Just keep an eye on this Edred. I will accept their oaths and see they are equipped with decent horses and weapons, but at the same time get some of the more experienced men in my gesith to check their abilities. I have a feeling in my bones that one day there is going to be a very awesome battle. I want every man in my army to be fit, healthy and fully trained with the weapons that suit him best. Call the witan for the morning then I will take their oaths before the four of you. And after that I am going to be crowned! I will not be held back any longer!' he said strongly.

Cerdic grinned at him. 'Of course not, sire!' he replied with his tongue in his cheek. 'Whoever would think such a thing!'

Aethelstan shook his head with amusement, slapped the nearby Ceorl on his back, then feeling a tremendous thirst, went to Edith's kitchen and hovered hopefully for some of her ale. Osburga took it out to him with a stool and he drank with appreciation, then lapsed into his own thoughts. He had never fully realised the obstructions that would be continually placed in his path, delaying his journey to Kingston. Perhaps once he was crowned, everyone would accept the situation and he could concentrate on the very important matter of uniting his England into one land, one people, one language, one currency, one strong race.

Edith watched him surreptitiously. There was a lot of truth in the comment Cerdic had made about this young king having so many problems just to wear a crown. Was it worth it? She didn't think so and was heartily glad she was not royal. The fact that Cerdic, with his fellow witan members, had been made an earldorman was more than rank enough. She watched him empty his tankard and took him out another one.

'Bless you, lady wife!' Aethelstan said with meaning. 'That first one did not even touch the sides!' Then he nodded at Rannulf being spoken to by Ceorl. 'Do you think that young man and your daughter may make a match?'

Edith hesitated. 'My daughter can be stubborn and pigheaded at times, sire, and I also fancy that young man has a mind of his own. Whether they are suitable I simply have no idea. I suppose only time will tell, but I do not want any divorces in this family. They are not only sordid but can get very acrimonious. And like all young people they can't be told, they know it all. They must learn from their mistakes, because I won't encourage a match and neither will her father. If anything should arise in the future then let it take place—in the future!' she said very coolly and firmly.

Aethelstan turned over these words, which echoed with wisdom, and he smiled up at her as she stood to one side, an empty tankard in one hand.

'Now, sire, if you'll forgive me, I have two very hungry churls to feed. I made them go wash and put on clean clothes. There is no reason for dirty habits, especially in my home!' and with a nod of respect she walked away.

Quite suddenly Aethelstan felt a little sympathy for these wandering churls. They had better obey this housewife or their life would be hell from a splendid lady wife called Edith.

FOUR

On the ride back from Kingston they were a large party and even a bit boisterous. The Archbishop of Canterbury had performed the dignified ceremony with Aethelstan sat on the royal Saxon stone, used for so many crownings in the past. There were still parts of the island that had not yet agreed to accept Aethelstan, and Sihtric was a very reluctant under-king at York. There was Constantine of the Scots as well as two large Welsh kings, with a number of smaller under-kings, to say nothing of the Celts near Exeter. It seemed an enormous task to try and persuade everyone to unite as one country, but if anyone could do it, it was King Aethelstan. The Great King Alfred had tried, as had his daughter the fighting Lady of Mercia. Even the devious King Edward had fought with this object in view, but to no avail at all. He supposed it went back so many years to when the island was held by various tribes, each of which guarded its boundaries jealously. He discounted any unity imposed by the Romans because that was sheer occupation by weight of numbers, with better trained and disciplined legionnaires.

Rannulf found himself riding with Osburga with rather mixed feelings. She was not backwards in coming forwards with questions.

'Are you ever going to marry?' she wanted to know.

'Who knows?' he shot back at her, then mollified his tone a little. 'If I did it'll not be in any hurry. My father did that and lived to regret it. I'm only eighteen, as far as I know and I have lots more learning to do with my work.'

Osburga was uncertain what to make of that. At nearly fifteen she was ready for marriage, but no one had really caught her attention, though Rannulf had started to become interesting. She must confide in her mother because they had a good, close relationship. She knew her father had developed considerable respect for the young scribe, so was it her being picky?

They arrived at their home base and all were amazed at how their new house had grown in their absence. Cerdic took the king around with pride. There was a very large hall with many sleeping chambers leading off and a fire at the end, but the cooking fire was in its own room.

'I like that!' Aethelstan remarked. 'Cuts out a fire risk with fats!'

'That's what we thought, sire!' Cerdic agreed with pride, because it had all been his design. The walls were, as usual, of substantial timber but all the floors were stone flagged. Once fresh rushes went down and weapons placed on the walls in patterns it would be a welcoming home. 'Ceorl is going to have the same design but smaller. We have both engaged reliable reeves for when we're away on your business, and I'm giving manumission to all my slaves so I can take their oaths as their lord. No more slaves for me at all and my joy agrees!'

Aethelstan smiled at his nickname for Edith but agreed it suited. 'Can I stay here when in the area?' he asked with his usual politeness.

'Of course! We have earmarked a chamber just for you!' and he strode forward, opened a door and the king stepped into a sunlit room with substantial shutters for the bad weather. 'This is just fine. Many thanks to both of you!'

It was later that two couriers arrived on sweaty, very tired horses, each of whom had been escorted by two warriors. Cerdic opened the letter addressed to him and passed the other to the king. He read rapidly and nodded with immense satisfaction.

'Sire! Another problem solved. Elfred did bolt to Normandy, got caught in a storm, soaked to his skin and retired to bed with someone. His breathing became very bad indeed and he simply turned his face to the wall and died.' Aethelstan was relieved.

Was there anyone else with ideas of coming after him? He wished he knew.

'My news is not so good,' he explained. 'This is from my sister. Sihtric has turned nasty. Repudiated her and Christianity, gone back to paganism but she says she doesn't think he has long to go. Very unhealthy colour. Anlaf might cause trouble for me as well as Olaf, the sons from his first marriage.'

Cerdic pulled a face. They sorted out one trouble and promptly acquired another. 'What do we know of either of them, sire?'

Aethelstan gave a shrug. 'Nothing much except they will be adult enough to cause trouble. Both of them too!'

'Sire!' a voice called. 'Another courier just ridden in!'

Both Aethelstan and Cerdic whipped around as the gesith came nearer in a protective half circle, but the new rider was so exhausted he hardly saw them and his horse staggered near to foundering from being so hard ridden.

Men sprang forward to help him as he fumbled in a pouch and brought out his message, which he passed to the king. Aethelstan checked the seal then broke it open and read swiftly as his lips tightened. 'Call the witan!' he snapped at Cerdic immediately.

The four of them hastily convened, and only when the king was ready did they sit with him on hastily acquired stools. He waved the letter at them.

'Sihtric is dead. This is from my sister, and Olaf Sigtryggson has proclaimed himself King of Northumbria, so that's it. War!' he grated.

Cerdic, Ceorl, Oswald and Egbert eyed each other, then waited for the king.

Aethelstan marshalled his thoughts into a coherent sequence of proposed activities. 'What we'll do is this. We'll march to war on that fool Olaf and trounce him on the battlefield once and for all. There will be spies around us. If you spot any don't halt them. Let them ride back with the news that the King of England is coming north with a mighty army!'

'When, sire?' the witan members chanted as one.

Aethelstan sat quietly thinking. 'When we are ready but without hurrying. We are going to be a mighty horde so no reeve will be able to feed us despite crossing through rich hundreds. We will have to take our own cattle with us to slaughter as and when we want the meat. The same with the horse herds. Drink will also be required so the logistics are going to take a little while to organise. Guards must be left here to protect the women, non-combatants and our homes.' He turned to Cerdic.

'This will be a good time to free your

slaves. Make them all gerburs, give them a few acres for a cow and growing their own food, and their duties for this exchange will be guardianship of the homes and women. The females will work inside under your good wife. Pick the best man out of them to be a kind of bailiff. Everywhere here will then be safe. One of you check our travelling tents are in good order. From today I'll move back into one myself to be like the men. Never let it be said I had to live under a roof while they only had their tents. Once you witan members are happy with all arrangements, then, and only then, do we march on Olaf. I guarantee the wait might drive him into a panic if nothing else!' Aethelstan grinned wolfishly. 'After I've thrashed Olaf I ride into York to my sister, though I think we may detect a hint she's found someone else, a Dane!'

Cerdic groaned. 'A Dane?'

'Relax! He is a Christian at least!' and Aethelstan explained further. 'A Christian Dane could be useful as my spy in York!'

The witan had not considered this but after rolling it around in their minds they all nodded sagaciously. What a cunning, farsighted king they had.

Once their meeting ended, the four of them bustled off attending to various tasks. Cerdic was perhaps the busiest as he called his slaves to him and explained in detail. Their joy was almost delirium and every man and woman came to swear an oath to Earldorman Cerdic.

Edith approved and so did Osburga, who was enlightened for her age. She had always thought people as slaves were so demeaned, which was why, she told herself, she was getting very interested in Rannulf. The trouble was he did not appear to notice her existence. This was not missed by Edith, who spoke gently to her.

'Remember, he has secured for himself a most prestigious position and is still learning. Be patient. Don't try and push anything!'

Osburga accepted her mother's gentle rebuke and knew she had not been charitable to start with. She vowed to be different without chasing. He had to, must, come after her. That was the law of nature.

Rannulf was fascinated with this turn of events. 'You will be with me at all times,' Ceorl explained. 'The witan do not fight. They have done their share in the past and are too old for active battle. You and I hold ourselves available for any written work the king might wish to have done, and the other witan members become our backup though their writing is pathetic!' he warned with a chuckle. He was going to enjoy some activity.

His mood was infectious throughout the large gathering as weapons were checked and sharpened and keen eyes examined the horse herd, rejecting any with possible suspect leg or hoof troubles.

Rannulf felt so incredibly happy. It was fantastic to think just how his life had changed, and he blessed the initiative that had sent him walking and wandering from York. That afternoon he heard the soft and gentle music from nearby and paused to listen with appreciation.

A wandering minstrel had sauntered into their camp, escorted by two guards, and he played to entertain and, they guessed, hopefully get a meal. His music was good so Rannulf repositioned where he stood to see better, and frowned. He stared hard to make sure then gritted his teeth while his mind revolved with worry and fear. He hesitated to step forward into the open while his heart pounded. He felt his stomach give a lurch and forced himself not to be sick. He threw a look around but there was no one near, not even his father. Everyone was entranced with the music, then the king called and Cerdic invited the minstrel inside the king's tent.

Rannulf stood frozen with total horror, unable to know what to do for the best. Sweat broke out on his forehead and his stomach gave another warning lurch from too much tension. The music went on and on and those warriors outside shouted their pleasure. Eventually it all stopped and the musician appeared carrying his reward, a generous bag of coins. He gave a general nod then calmly strolled away escorted to the correct path by a gesith guard.

Rannulf acted. He charged forward like a mad bull and burst into the king's tent, nearly sending Cerdic flying where he had been chatting with the king.

Cerdic jumped with shock. 'What the hell do you think you're doing barging in like this? How dare you? Get out! You've obviously become too big for your breeches. This writing has gone to your head. Now OUT I say!' he roared.

Aethelstan stood equally astonished and displeased. Rannulf ignored Cerdic and faced his king. His expression was one of total misery.

'Sire! Sire! I know who that was. Be careful!'

Aethelstan was dumbfounded, at a loss for words. Cerdic lost his temper, grabbed Rannulf's left arm to drag him outside, but the younger man resisted, then slung a punch at Cerdic's jaw. The older was totally unprepared and went flying backwards to land on his seat.

'Why, you . . . !' Cerdic roared with rage.

Rannulf ignored him and turned his white face but with sweaty forehead to the king. 'I know who that was, sire. It was Anlaf!'

'Eh?'

'It was, sire!'

'Why the hell didn't you say so? I could have captured him,' Aethelstan shouted, his own temper going sky high.

Rannulf nearly burst into tears. 'But I

couldn't, sire! I gave my oath to him when at York, because Sihtric wouldn't see me. I have given my oath to you here. If you learned I'd broken the first oath you'd never trust me with the second!' he protested vehemently.

Aethelstan paused to reflect. He shook his head, suddenly appreciating the young man's quandary, and flashed a questioning look at Cerdic, who stood flatfooted with shock.

Aethelstan took a deep breath and shook his head. 'I do take your point,' he finally agreed, 'but it leaves me the loser!' he said coldly.

Rannulf was distraught with misery. How was it possible that his wonderful life here could collapse so suddenly? He also knew he could not stop now.

He dropped to his knees and placed his hands crossed on his chest in abject supplication. 'Whatever you do to me, sire, please, I beg of you, do not sleep in your tent tonight!'

'What!' Aethelstan roared. 'This is too, too much. Get him out!'

Cerdic stepped forward furious with Rannulf, for whom he had started to have considerable respect.

'No! No, sire! You sleep in your tent tonight and you'll be a very dead king by the morning!'

'Out!' Aethelstan bellowed but frowned as he saw tears pour freely down the young man's face with his passion.

Cerdic grabbed him by the arm, hauled him to his feet, dragged him outside and saw Ceorl. 'Take him away and give him the thrashing he has earned!'

Ceorl was staggered and at a loss for words. He could not last remember when he had seen his friend so angry and he had heard the king's voice raised in fury. 'Home!' he barked. 'And explain yourself to me!'

Cerdic rejoined the king and shook his head ruefully. His shoulders slumped. Aethelstan stood thoughtfully looking at the tent's rather dirty walls.

'We'll teach him,' he said slowly with a frown. The young man's tears had been so genuine. 'I will move into another tent, then in the morning that young man will see what a fool he has been. A good object lesson!'

Cerdic nodded though did not wholly agree. He was too furious with Rannulf to think straight.

Ceorl slammed his door shut and turned to berate his son, but Rannulf had slumped forward over the table while he cried like a child. 'I'm right,' he sobbed. 'I know I am!'

Ceorl slumped down opposite, confused and upset. 'Tell me your story. Every word. Miss nothing!'

Struggling to control his emotions Rannulf went back to his early days in York. 'I didn't like him from the start. He's devious and untrustworthy. That's when I heard King

Aethelstan was at Tamworth a lot, but he'd gone when I arrived so I carried on walking here until I found him. I then gave him my oath. I'm allowed to change if I want to, can't I?'

'Of course you are, though it's not common practice. Now go on. What exactly happened after you'd burst into the king's tent?' Ceorl persisted.

When Rannulf finished Ceorl eyed him. 'Go and wash your face,' he said not unkindly.

'Are you going to thrash me?'

'No, but I'm going to improve your manners a bit with discussion. No one bursts into the king's private tent. Why! He might have had a female in there!' he lied to drive home his point.

Rannulf shook his head wearily. 'I just did not know what to do,' he explained again plaintively. He had a feeling tonight was going to be sleepless, he was so worked up he could not think straight.

Cerdic was still in a temper. 'If his father doesn't thrash him I will, sire!' he raged.

Aethelstan shook his head. 'I know in an equal fight Ceorl could never match you, but I think it would be a shame to end a friendship over this. We'll do it my way. I'll move but keep it quiet. I think I saw a fighting bishop hovering with his mercenaries, looking for food and a bed for the night. You'd better go and see to him. Can't have the Church upset!'

69

Rannulf tossed and turned for most of the night but did drop off an hour before dawn. He awoke with a violent start. There was a cacophony outside. Men's voices bellowing. Loud shouts. General uproar. The noise was outrageous. He forced himself off his cot as Ceorl appeared.

'What the hell . . . ?' Ceorl began and went outside, a still sleepy Rannulf at his heels.

The bishop's mercenaries, in both rage and shock, stamped around, waving their weapons and bellowing at Cerdic who had just appeared. Then the king came, dressed just in his sleeping tunic and small clothes. Unwashed, hair uncombed, as confused as the rest of them. They all watched Cerdic go into the tent with the mercenary leader then come out, white-faced with total horror. He went up to his king.

'The bishop is dead, sire. A knife straight in his heart!'

Aethelstan stamped forward, elbowed everyone out of his way, entered and stared down. He bent and looked carefully then slowly straightened and faced Cerdic who had followed him. There was just one clean wound. A knife had penetrated unerringly into the bishop's heart and surprisingly little blood showed. Death had been instantaneous.

'That was meant for me,' Aethelstan said soberly, still in deep shock. 'The boy has been right all along. I have some grovelling to do—

70

and you also!' he growled harshly. 'I'll get washed and dressed. Find out who the sentry was here last night. These mercenaries are under my orders for the time being. You—control your men!' he rasped at the obvious leader. 'Name?'

'Burhred, sire. I confirm I am the leader!'

Aethelstan turned and hurried back to make himself presentable, while his mind revolved. He could not remember last receiving a bigger shock. He also reeled with considerable guilt for the way Rannulf had been treated.

Cerdic bellowed and looked around at the huge gathering, all murmuring in disbelief. 'Who was sentry here last night?' he roared.

Hoel stepped forward with shame and horror. 'Me, Lord!'

Cerdic eyed him. He was a gesith member in his early thirties and a good fighter, but this . . . ? 'Speak!' he bellowed.

Hoel took a deep breath. 'I was standing just there—' and he pointed. 'When suddenly a small thin man appeared seemingly from nowhere. I'd not heard him. He was wearing very soft shoes and had not made a sound. He was drinking or, at least, had a beaker with ale in it. He offered it to me, said he'd had enough, would I like to share and I was pleased to as the supper meat had left me thirsty. I did think it had a bit of a funny taste but I just thought it was ale, which had not stood long enough to mature. I emptied it, then the next thing I knew the noise here woke me. I'd been sleeping on the ground. I can't even remember lying down!' he finished miserably.

Cerdic saw it all, so did the rest of the witan who stood around. 'Drugged!' Cerdic grated, then his wits snapped into action. 'Show me exactly where he stood!'

Hoel hurried to obey, knowing he was in the most awful trouble. Cerdic was no expert tracker, but he was above average. He studied the indentations in the soft earth, then stiffened and poked with one boot.

'Been here a while, just waiting. Look! He was taken short and had to crap. Get two good hounds, put them on leashes and bring them,' he ordered harshly.

When they came he spoke to their handler, then the mercenary leader Burhred, just as the king reappeared. Washed, dressed, tidy but still in shock.

'Let the hounds get this scent. It should still be fresh enough, then follow. You mercenaries do the same but keep back from the hounds. I want this man. Dead or alive!' he thundered. 'Now get!'

After deep sniffing the hounds understood and one let out an enthusiastic howl and the party moved off.

Aethelstan turned. He could feel eyes boring through his tunic from Rannulf and Ceorl. He stepped forward to them.

'I was very, very wrong. Will you forgive your king and take to wear this bracelet as my token.' He passed to Rannulf a magnificent gold and silver bracelet intricately carved. 'You have saved England as well as me. My debt to you is—enormous! I have learned my lesson. I will never doubt your word again, young man! Ceorl, be proud of your son, who had the guts to stand against the temper of me and Cerdic.'

Rannulf went scarlet with embarrassment as the king slipped the valuable bracelet on his right arm then turned to the fascinated onlookers. 'Let all know, men and women, that the King of England is forever in this young man's debt!'

There was a roar of approval from the spectators and Rannulf looked around in panic, saw Osburga and shot a helpless look at her. She understood in a flash, realised his acute embarrassment, felt for him and stepped forward to face the king.

'Sire, I'd like to be taken a little walk. May I?' and very pointedly she slipped her hand through Rannulf's left arm, then daringly she winked with her left eye. Aethelstan smiled with gentle amusement and was also quick in understanding. Rannulf was so embarrassed at all this attention. He did not know where to look and his face was as scarlet as an autumn berry.

'Off you both go, but keep well away from

the hounds' tracking line. I want that man!' Aethelstan told all of them.

Rannulf and Osburga, she clinging fast to him, bowed their heads then turned and sauntered away. 'Bless you!' Rannulf whispered to her. 'I couldn't have stood much more of that, I'd rather take the thrashing,' he joked lightly.

'I respect you, very much so!' she said honestly then paused and looked into his eyes.

Rannulf again felt a bit helpless but knew he must give honesty in return. 'I have fancied you for a while,' he said slowly, 'but it's only fair to tell you I won't think of marriage for another year.'

Osburga frowned. She had been courted before and rejected a number of proposals but this was a new experience.

'Why one year?'

Rannulf struggled to explain. 'I've become a good scribe but have more I've given myself to learn. You see my father is far from being young and we both know there is going to be a lot of riding coming up for the king. I want to be good enough to take his place so he can stay in his home. Also I have no house of my own and not the means to get one built yet. I know Father's house, when finished, is going to be big enough for him and my family when I have one, but I insist upon a year's wait so I may consolidate myself at my work, which is fascinating. It also means that my wife will have to accept long absences with my work as the king's scribe—just as your mother has had to deal with equally long absences. How would you feel about such a life?'

Osburga smiled at him. 'I would understand and accept, as has my mother. I would wait too.'

'You would!' and Rannulf's heart swelled with gratitude. This sensible, down-to-earth girl would make a perfect, understanding wife. 'Then as soon as possible I will give you my token!' he promised.

'And I'll wear it with pride!' This was a rare young man and her heart throbbed with joy. How wrong she had been initially. Then she stiffened. Both of the hounds set up a fearful baying, which came back to them through the trees and shrubs.

'They've got him!' Rannulf cried and spun around. 'Back!'

They ran back, hand in hand, as Cerdic sat with his fellow witan members. Off to one side stood a miserable Hoel. Cerdic beckoned him forward with a stern look, and Hoel placed himself before Mercia's four wise men.

'Your conduct has been a disgrace,' Cerdic growled at him. 'You are suspended from the gesith for two months, downgraded to that of ordinary foot soldier. Now get out of our sight!' Egbert barked.

As Hoel departed, head lowered, Oswald spoke for them all. 'The other men will give him hell. I know one thing, if he ever does sentry duty again I bet a mouse won't fool him and pass by!'

There was a flurry of activity and shouting and the mercenaries returned dragging with them a small man whom the eager hounds had mauled so he bled copiously. They flung him down before the witan and Aethelstan, who had appeared.

'Strip him!' Cerdic barked. With roughness the mercenaries did so, removing a purse from around a scraggy neck and handing it to Cerdic. He peered inside and his eyebrows shot up, then he handed the purse and its contents back to the mercenary leader.

'Anlaf sent you! And you have been paid in advance as this purse's contents show!' Cerdic accused hotly.

The man said nothing but his eyes rolled with fear and panic as he licked dry lips. The mercenary leader kicked his ribs. 'Answer the lord!'

The killer gave a little nod. He knew he was doomed. He had murdered. Cerdic snorted. 'Take him away and do with him as you wish. It was your lord he killed and a bishop too—' He paused and shot a look at the king. 'If you want to give fresh oaths . . . ?'

'We do, Lord and sire!' Burhred, the leader, spoke for them all.

His rough and ready motley of near rogues obeyed him to the last letter, because he was

76

capable and harsh enough to thrash all of them. For this he had their utmost respect. He had also proved he was not ungenerous where loot was concerned, which was what their life was all about. Cerdic waved a hand and they dragged the killer away to dispense their own, harsh justice.

FIVE

Ceorl had not thought of that. 'No money? My fault. I'll get wages arranged but what do you suddenly want money for?'

Rannulf explained and Ceorl paused, thinking. 'Are you sure she's the one? You lack experience.' He spoke carefully.

'I'm sure, and she understands I'll be away often with my work. Her mother knows what that's like and they're two of a real kind!'

Ceorl had to agree with such an observation. He turned and went to his own chamber, and after a few minutes returned. He held out a necklace of gold with small Christian symbols attached. 'It was my mother's,' he explained. 'It's your token for her. Now go and take it because the witan is meeting. There is much to organise!'

Aethelstan sat in with his advisers, though it was Cerdic who led the conversation as the senior.

'Take the oaths of those mercenaries first, sire. Their leader is called Burhred and he's a tough one. They all are come to that but they'll be good fighters. That breed are!'

'Arrange it with just a short ceremony. I want to get off after Olaf as soon as possible, but I plan to move slowly, like a tide coming. Unstoppable! That should panic Olaf. Also I want the men as fresh as possible. Those mercenaries are to be split into two groups. They can fight each side of my gesith but they'll do as they're told,' Aethelstan warned. 'You non-combatants will keep well to the rear and out of any possible trouble, but still arm yourselves in case any hotheads break through. I think stabbing spears will be the best weapons for you. Rannulf will stay with you as well. I've watched him practise with weapons but he's not very good at all!' Aethelstan told Ceorl.

Rannulf went scarlet with this truth. His weapon was the written word.

Ceorl hastened to his beloved son's defence. 'Probably because he was a slave.' No owner in his right mind encouraged fighting skill in slaves.

That made sense to all of them. 'Scouts have been seen watching us at a distance but they've been left alone,' Cerdic said.

'Good!' Aethelstan replied. 'We'll move when you're satisfied the logistics are in order. Plenty of pack animals for the tents and other equipment. Make sure each man checks the weapon he intends to use. I want a sharp, hard victory so the news can spread everywhere. Other kings might then come in with us,' and he turned to Cerdic. 'After the fight I'll be riding into York. I intend to start minting my own coins marked Rex Tot Brit, King of the whole of Britain. Later on I shall issue other charters for York, not Yorvik. English is to be spoken, though if the Danes have particular customs I don't mind these. They will eventually die out, taken over by English ones. On our return I want to move my court to the royal Saxon palace at Pucklechurch, and I want personal invitations to go to continental noble families for my other half sisters. I will also be happy to foster at my court Alan of Brittany and the son of Haakon of Norway. I want a large, cultured court where all are welcomed, especially scholars from all countries, whether they be Germans, Irish, Franks, Bretons, Italians and even Icelanders. All are to be welcomed.' He paused to look around.

Ceorl and Rannulf were writing furiously. So much to do and organise.

'As you know, I collect relics for the Holy Church so agents can travel around the continent looking for me. Let the word spread I pay generously. The same with books.'

Cerdic started to chuckle and the others looked at him. 'I think the coming fight is going to be the easiest task!'

'Now when can I march?' Aethelstan asked.

The witan exchanged looks, did some rapid calculating and Cerdic spoke for them all. 'In three days' time, sire!'

'The sooner the better!' Aethelstan said firmly and touched the precious sword from his beloved aunt. 'It's time this was blooded!' and he paused: 'So far it's been mere decoration.'

As Aethelstan left them Cerdic spoke to Ceorl. 'I need a little while with your son. Can you manage?'

Ceorl nodded and gestured to Rannulf, who obediently followed the witan leader until they were privately alone.

Cerdic didn't beat about the bush. 'I owe you my apology, young man. I hope you will accept this from a rapidly aging warrior?'

'Of course, my lord, now I wish to have words with Osburga in private!' he said equally blunt.

Cerdic waved a hand to his new home where the freed slaves were working with great enthusiasm. Osburga spotted him and ran out beaming. Rannulf grabbed her and took her aside and produced that given to him by his father. He showed it to her then fastened it around her neck.

'With this I plight thee my troth. Will you accept?'

Osburga looked at the beautiful necklace and her eyes sparkled. She had never expected

80

such grandeur. 'Of course I do,' then her eyes twinkled. 'Just you try and take it from me!' she teased then kissed him ardently.

They spent a few minutes together watched by a delighted Edith and Cerdic, then Rannulf broke free, turned and walked back to Cerdic.

'When the king goes into York I wish to be with him!' he stated.

'What on earth for? Ceorl will be there to take any notes. I'd have thought that would be the last place you'd wish to visit.'

'That's just it. I want to see if my old slave master is there and see if he can remember my natural parents. It's all a long time ago but I feel I must find out what I can for Osburga,' he explained quietly.

Cerdic applauded the proposed action but doubted the young man could possibly learn anything after so many years. 'I'll see what I can arrange!' he promised.

Later on, in the privacy of their night chamber, they talked about him. 'Right from the start, I saw something in him I liked!' Edith said thoughtfully.

'You were ahead of me then, my joy!' Cerdic confessed. 'Now no more talking. I've two days' work to do tomorrow then we march to battle.'

* * *

Aethelstan looked ahead and studied the

terrain. He had dressed very carefully that morning. Next to his skin he wore a very fine silk, long-sleeved tunic. Over this went a leather tunic, thin but strong enough to retard most bruising, and finally he wore top-quality chain mail, which reached to his knees. His helmet completely covered his head, leaving just a little portion of neck. Before fastening his cross garters his legs had also been metal padded. He held his shield, again of strong metal, so its tip rested on the earth while he looked around.

The ground ahead was fairly flat and the enemy was lined up ready with someone prancing at the front, bellowing personal challenges. He ignored them. His flanks were clear except there were a few trees to the left.

'Send a patrol through those trees to make sure the enemy's reinforcements won't come at us from that direction!' he ordered, and a mounted patrol galloped off.

'Right! Let's start!' and Aethelstan advanced on foot, withdrawing his wonderful sword, his gesith on each side. They would protect his flanks but leave him free to fight from the front. The patrol returned and their leader shook his head.

'Just two medicine women waiting, sire!'

Aethelstan marvelled. Just how did these amazing women turn up when they knew their services were to be needed? It had always baffled him, though he knew it was said they went back centuries with their knowledge to the old Druids. He looked ahead. The enemy had started to advance, so did he.

Within a few paces the warriors met and there was uproar as blade met blade and voices were raised in bellows of triumph or pain. Aethelstan concentrated on his front, wielding his sword, trying to pick out the other king. He dodged, ducked with his shield aloft and his sword plunging at or carving any opposing men. Very soon everyone was sweating with the sheer exertion of wielding heavy weapons, and the gesith was hard pressed to keep on their king's flanks. A battleaxe descended. Aethelstan's shield met it and was promptly split in two, but the king's sword plunged into that warrior's heart. The gesith man on his left tossed his shield to his king and took one from his immediate left, each man passing it in a smooth movement, long practised. The one left shieldless jumped back two paces and one from the rear was hastily thrust into his hand. Immediately he stepped back into the gesith line again, striking with his javelin, snarling his bloodlust.

Aethelstan fought as if possessed, which he was, driven by his royal blood and kingship. He took care where he placed his feet, because men were down near him, and once he did stumble over a headless torso, but regained his balance. On and on, strike, maim or kill. Where was Olaf, he asked himself?

But that king's helmet no longer showed. He snarled again, his handsome faced turned into a ferocious mask. Then it happened so suddenly he was surprised. Olaf's men broke, turned, started a retreat, which turned into an immediate, uncontrollable rout.

Aethelstan paused and was pleased to see his breathing had only increased slightly. His superb fitness had paid off. He halted, his sword dripping blood copiously, then calmly bent and wiped the blade on a dead man's tunic before sheathing it. His gesith copied but were still wary of any last-minute rush by madmen, but there weren't any left.

The witan came forward, including Rannulf, each had been ready with a stabbing spear and shield.

'Short, sharp and very sweet!' Aethelstan said to the five men and flashed his teeth in a wild grin. 'My aunt's sword has been well and truly baptised!'

The earth in front of them was left a mass of wounded and dying men from both sides. From his peripheral vision Aethelstan watched two medicine women appear, one very old, the other much younger, each carrying a pouch with medicinal herbs. They parted and started to do what they could for the desperate men crying for aid.

Aethelstan's chain mail was covered in others' blood, and he turned to Cerdic. 'After this the men are to be well and truly rested and refreshed. Send out a scout to see where Olaf has bolted. I'm going to wash and change, then ride into York to see my sister.'

Cerdic hastily explained Rannulf's wish and the king nodded agreement. Just then there was a hoarse bellow and Ceorl rushed forward, grabbing the younger medicine woman, who was startled. He spun her around and peered into bright, blue eyes. Her hair was tied loosely at the back, as fair coloured as ripe corn.

Ceorl snatched her to him, then planted kisses on her lips. 'It's her!' The young woman struggled furiously, twisted one foot and kicked Ceorl's shin. He gave a sharp cry and released her. Quick as a flash she withdrew her scramasax, and holding the dagger for an underhand upward thrust waved it at him.

'Try that again and I'll gut you!' she screeched.

Aethelstan stood in shocked amazement, as did the older woman. Ceorl looked around frantically.

'It is her! My Judith. I've looked for you for years!!' he blurted out at her.

'Never met you before in my life!' she retorted.

Aethelstan flashed a look at the older woman and stepped aside where she joined him. 'Have you any idea, good mother, what this is all about, please?' he asked politely.

She knew whom he was and like all of her kind was not particularly impressed with either rank or status. He was simply another fighting warrior who bled like the rest.

'Not in the slightest!'

Ceorl thrust himself forward and garbled out the story of his terrible divorce and how he had seen Judith for only a handful of days before she vanished. Over the years he had never stopped looking for her. He turned beseeching sheep's eyes on his king.

'Do something, please, sire!'

Aethelstan caught his breath, flashed a look with a shake of his head at the older woman, but was at a loss exactly what to do next. She was quicker and beckoned Judith to the other side. 'He has always fancied you, it seems!'

Judith was a practical, down-to-earth female. 'Tough! He's not much to look at as a warrior!'

Aethelstan overheard and joined them. 'He isn't a warrior. He is a highly valued king's scribe. An earldorman with a very high wergild!'

The old woman pricked up her ears and studied the quivering Ceorl, who was so agitated his eyes glistened with emotion. She took Judith away four steps.

'Handsome is as handsome does,' she commenced. 'You are very good with healing plants but think long term. One day I will know my time has arrived and I will depart quietly and you will never know. I shall go to a private place about which you also know

86

nothing. I shall close the door and die alone. Is this how you want to go when you appear to have a chance to elevate yourself in comfort and security?' she asked bluntly.

Judith had to shake her head. 'But I can't even remember him!' she protested in her defence.

The old woman walked back to the king. 'She can read and write. Let him court her through letters over the months. If anything happens after that—' and she let the sentence hang fire.

Aethelstan gave a sigh of relief. 'Splendid idea, good mother! This one is beyond me. Battle is much simpler!' he smiled down at her. She was small and incredibly old. 'Did you hear that, Ceorl? You will court the young lady by letter until she says otherwise!' and this was a harsh order.

Ceorl would have agreed to just about anything. He approached Judith again and gingerly took one hand. 'Please?' he begged.

Judith knew she was flattered by such attention but also the old woman's words had registered with her. She stared at him frankly. An earldorman! A valued king's scribe! Slowly she nodded agreement. It would take weeks for a letter to reach him so she would have plenty of time to change her mind and vanish if she chose. She gave another brief nod, then turned to assist at the older woman's side. There were the dying to be put out of their misery. They came first.

Ceorl jigged with delight, hit Cerdic on one shoulder, beamed broadly at his king then spotted Burhred returning from the battlefield.

'Looting?' he asked quietly. 'Please may I see?'

Burhred hesitated, then opened a large pouch purse, which was half filled with rings, brooches and coins. Ceorl peered inside, delicately removing one brooch. It was round, silver and decorated with a Celtic cross.

'Take it if you fancy it. I'll find plenty more!' Burhred said generously.

Ceorl dived for his own neck purse and opened the drawstring. 'I'll buy it. It's for a lady. I can't donate something given to me, can I?' he asked reasonably.

Burhred was a hard-bitten, grizzled man of the world. 'As you like!' and he peered in the proffered purse and extracted some coins, then handed the brooch over.

Ceorl grabbed it and bustled over to Judith again. She was helping a man to die with a special drink, a warrior whose arm and shoulder had been cleaved away with a battleaxe. She frowned at being interrupted. Ceorl had enough sense to control his emotions. He just leaned forward and with delicacy pinned the brooch on her front, then turned to retrace his steps, feeling as if he were floating on summer clouds.

Aethelstan rolled his eyes at Cerdic, shook

his head, moved to a waiting horse, then rode away to wash and change before riding into York as the victorious king.

*   *   *

Rannulf was stunned. The noise! The people! York had never been so crowded and active in his younger days. He rode at the rear of the king's retinue. Around Aethelstan was a small gesith with Ceorl and Cerdic as they moved slowly forward to the palace.

Rannulf had been granted permission to rejoin the group at the palace, so he rode slowly, eyes everywhere. He heard the city referred to as Yorvik, and English rarely spoken. There was so much trading activity and people stared at the conquering king's progress with some interest, but most of them were far more intent upon the important business of trade. He halted at Fleshammels, which was the street of the butchers. Meat was displayed from every window, even the wide ones upstairs. He remembered from old that sometimes the smell was repugnant on hot days, but it was the only way for the butchers to display their wares. Then the city was often referred to by its old English name of Fofbrwic, which simply meant meats-wild-boar-town. He almost preferred the old Norse name of Yorvik, which translated to Horse Bay. The city buzzed with tremendous activity

89

now as then. Did trades people never sleep?

By standing in his stirrup he extended his view, then frowned as he saw an area roped off with horses for sale. He pushed his way through patiently then sat quietly and stared. Yes! It was him, though a much older version.

The man in his early fifties realised he was under observation and pushed his way forward. 'Want to buy a horse, Lord?'

Rannulf stared down at him. He was finely dressed with a splendid green tunic of quality material, which matched the rest of his attire. He sat on his horse, reins in his left hand and, on the right arm, the magnificent bracelet from the king.

None of this was missed by the horse dealer. 'Any particular type of horse, Lord?'

'Information first,' Rannulf said quietly. 'I thought you used to sell slaves?'

The man nodded. 'I did, but gave it up. Too long to wait to make decent money on them, so it's horses only now, Lord!'

Rannulf nodded a little. 'Tell me, but cast your mind back some years. Do you remember breeding a slave called Rannulf, who worked with your horses and who eventually bought his freedom from you?'

The dealer frowned, thinking back. Now why did such an important lord want to know? He dared not question. He flogged his mind into action. Memories began to return and suddenly he brightened and nodded.

'I do now, Lord. I'd forgotten all about him. I wonder if he still lives.' But that was rhetorical, not genuine curiosity.

'Yes, I do, as you can see!' Rannulf replied in a quiet voice.

The dealer looked up at this very important lord, frowned and struggled to understand. He knew he was with the king's retinue so what was his game? He hastily ran through mental permutations but ended up none the wiser and continued to stare upwards in obvious confusion and bewilderment.

'I am Rannulf, as you called me!'

The dealer tried to collect suddenly scattered wits, frowned, stared hard, shook his head then lifted both hands in supplication.

'If you say so, Lord!' was all he could manage.

'I mean it. I've come up in life. I am a king's scribe. I insist upon knowing my breeding because I have a reason!'

The dealer began to understand he was hearing the truth, so he closed his eyes and forced himself to think back down the years. Memories returned. He opened his eyes wide, looked up at the young lord again, then began to speak.

'It is all coming back, Lord. Your mother was a small thin girl. I shouldn't have bred from her because she had narrow hips. Never got over the confinement. Now your father was different. He had been a free churl but ran up enormous debts and was threatened with action if he didn't clear them. To do this he was left with no alternative but to sell himself into slavery. That's how I ended up buying him as a stud for breeding, because he looked so healthy and was adult.'

'Why such debt?' Rannulf asked, puzzled. A free churl to do that?

'Drink!' the dealer replied bluntly. 'I had my work cut out to keep him sober as a slave. He'd always find ways to get hold of ale. Such a waste of a life because he was a fine, strapping young fellow!'

'Where is he now?'

'Well and truly dead! I sent him and another out for boar because I fancied some of that meat roasted, but he must have been half drunk again. His spear missed. The boar did not. The other man climbed a tree to safety. When the boar went and he came down your father had bled to death. His name was Alcium, I think.'

Rannulf silently turned it all over in his mind. 'Alcium—from where?'

'Mercia, Lord.'

Rannulf opened his own neck purse and handed over a coin, then without another word or gesture he turned his horse to walk thoughtfully in the direction of the palace. At least he now knew and it wasn't as bad as he'd thought it would be. All because of ale! He made a personal vow, there and then, for the rest of his life he would treat ale with the greatest respect. He kept his vow.

Inside the palace Ceorl and Cerdic greeted him and he explained what he'd learned.

'Well!' Ceorl said. 'You come from good stock!'

'The best!' Cerdic agreed.

'I must tell Osburga!' Rannulf said firmly.

'You may have a wait. The king's business comes first!' Cerdic reminded him swiftly. 'He wants Olaf once and for all, remember!'

'And I second that, son. Osburga must wait!' Ceorl added sternly.

'The king is with his sister now!' Cerdic explained.

Aethelstan smiled gently at his full sister. 'Tell me all, please!'

'Well, brother king. You made a real mess of this one. Sihtric was the most odious man and cruel with it. I found that out on the ride back after our wedding. He kept leaning over to pinch me and make me cry. And as for our first night, it was hideous. He said he'd make me beg for mercy. He did not and as he left he hit me. The same thing on the second night, but not on the third.'

She pulled aside a delicate silk robe over her long gown and showed him her dagger. 'I said if he hit me again I'd cut his throat as he slept. That did it. He left me alone but his language was foul as well as his attitude. That's when he repudiated me and Christianity.'

'You should have sent for me!'

'There was no need. He was unhealthy and started going downhill before my eyes. I was pleased to become a widow.'

'I'm so sorry. I had no idea, sis!'

She fixed him with a stern regal look. 'I hope you pick better for my sisters. It's easy for you men. You just take, but we females have to give!' she rebuked with harshness unusual for her. 'Now I pick my own man, brother king!' she warned. 'Or else!'

'What about this Dane?'

'He's nice, kind and gentle, but after my experience with Sihtric I'm in no hurry, I warn you, brother king!' she said firmly and paused. 'I know perfectly well sisters and half sisters are bargaining pieces for a king for alliances, but this time think long term and consider us females!' she rebuked coldly. 'I alone will have the final say. Not you! It may be the Dane. I can't say right now. He's a nice man but I demand time to get over that horrible Sihtric!' and her voice rang harsh with ice.

Aethelstan cringed with embarrassment and knew he had not bothered to investigate as he should. That mistake would not be made a second time. 'I'm sorry, sis. I promise that won't happen again!' and he meant it. What his sister had said was true. The female had to give all the time. It was so much easier for a male. He went scarlet with guilt and embarrassment and vowed in the future he would be a lot more circumspect with possible matrimonial selections. She changed her tone. Her point had been made and struck home with a vengeance, because her brother, whom she secretly adored, was a very good, kind man. He would not make a second mistake of such nature.

'Olaf is weak, but watch out for Anlaf,' she told him, now going out of her way to help him. 'He's the bad one to cause trouble!' she warned sincerely.

'He has already tried it on,' Aethelstan explained in enormous detail. 'I was a lucky man that night. It could so easily have been me with the knife in the heart, except for a brave young man who had the guts to stand up to me!'

She was deeply shocked. 'I didn't think he'd stoop that low. Where is he now? Over in Dublin I guess, because don't forget their king has kinship links with Northumbria. What a miracle you did as that young scribe advised!'

He nodded with chagrin. 'I had to eat a large dose of humble pie,' he admitted heavily, 'but I've been forgiven. I now feel in my bones this scribe is a dynamic young man going places. I'm glad he's on my side!' and he threw her a rueful grin. 'I have to go soon, to chase Olaf, then there are other areas to visit, but I'll be back here as soon as I can. I intend to establish a mint here with my own coins to start with. Take care, darling sister, but I do have to consider other noble families on the continent! It is vital I can turn to allies. Remember Grandfather made alliances whenever he could. I'm thinking of Otto, Duke of Saxony first of all, and French royalty. You two sisters could travel together and found your own dynasties! Your children would grow up royal and powerful, allied to us here. Grandfather Alfred would most certainly approve!' he wheedled hopefully.

Eadgyth gave him a sharp look then a tiny shake of her head. 'Kings!' she said slowly, not without a touch of sorrow. 'And leave our land. Easy for you to say and do.'

'Whatever I do or plan is for our country,' he replied gently. He would rather have her acceptance than use kingly force.

'I'll think about this,' she told him slowly. She knew there would be no Dane for her. She and all of her sisters were royal pawns. Their lives never their own because of their regal birth. She managed a wan smile, which he accepted with a huge sigh of relief. This had gone much better than he had dared to hope.

'Thank you, darling sister. I promise you'll not be the loser, and I mean what I say!' he vowed.

It was a thoughtful king who joined his party and slowly rode back to the battlefield. In many ways he felt deep sorrow for his beautiful sisters, but that was their role in regal life.

Cerdic flashed a questioning look at Ceorl,

but they said nothing. Their king was entitled to his off moments like the rest of them. Then Aethelstan realised he was being unusually taciturn to men upon whom he relied so much. He gestured for them to ride with him and related his sister's comments.

'The other noble families and my other sisters can all meet at Pucklechurch when I've sorted out Olaf. Rannulf! Give me your news!'

Rannulf hastened to comply and his king listened intently. 'All because of drink,' he murmured thoughtfully. 'Let this man's fate be a lesson to all of us!' and he smiled at Rannulf. 'You must feel happier knowing more about your breeding. What's this? Who is coming?'

Cerdic recognised one of their scouts, who brought his horse to a slithering halt. 'We have found him, sire. Olaf I mean. He has bolted to take refuge with King Constantine of the Scots!'

'Where exactly?' Aethelstan asked quickly.

'At his rock fortress at Dunnottar, sire!'

'Is that so?' said Aethelstan. 'I think we will have to pay this fortress a visit when the men are thoroughly rested and well fed. You witan men, I want to know how many killed, injured or maimed, including those mercenaries, especially among my gesith. Let that Hoel come back now. I saw him from my eye corner fighting like a man gone berserk. He's paid!' he said dryly. 'And send a messenger to your homes to let the women know all is well.' He paused. 'I'll speak to those medicine women to learn if any of the injured are borderline cases. Come! Let us ride. We all have plenty to do!'

SIX

Aethelstan found the older medicine woman and waited politely for her to finish sending a man to permanent sleep with one of her painless but lethal drinks.

'Many more like that, old mother?'

She did not like being interrupted, but could understand the gist of his question. Judith came over and he smiled winningly at her.

'I hope you've not changed your mind at writing to my scribe, or else I'll not get much work out of him!' he said gently. She was not exactly beautiful but she did have winning ways about her and was obviously full of spirit. Her eyes were so blue he was almost mesmerised by their wonderful colour. She had washed dirt and bloodstains from her hair and it glistened brightly like fresh corn. Dressed in tunic and trousers down to very practical boots, he was a bit amused to see she wore her scramasax in a prominent position. One snatch and her dagger would be out and she had already demonstrated she knew how to use it with the upward gutting blow.

'I'll write, though about what I don't

98

know,' Judith said slowly. She had given much thought to the scribe and by racking her brains had, just, managed to remember a distraught young man being divorced and taken to task by some elders. She acknowledged she was flattered by his attention. At the same time, the old mother's words had gone home. Did *she* wish to end her dying days alone in some obscure hut? No, she did not think so at the moment, though she was sufficiently worldly wise to know circumstances could alter situations. Although the scribe cut a poor figure against a warrior he was an earldorman with a high wergild. This was so important in their modern society.

'Just a simple personal message would give him great pleasure,' Aethelstan added, 'even if you only talk about the flowers you have seen!' he teased gently.

Her laugh was low and throaty. She liked this king, this man. What was his lady like, she wondered.

The old woman decided to break up what looked like turning into a mutual admiration society. 'There will be some more to die in the next day or night. We can do little for them. Wounds from battleaxes are too vicious. Some will also get the stinking disease,' she added and looked around. Most of the dead had been pulled to one side and it seemed the looting had ceased.

Aethelstan nodded soberly. It was a proven

fact that many battle wounds turned an ugly stinking black mess, which gave enormous pain and from which there was no hope of recovery. It was known this was caused by dirt getting deep into a wound and, for some reason, it always became worse when this included soil.

'Your payment, good mother?' he asked and reached for his own neck purse, removed it, opened the drawer cord and offered it to her. She hesitated only a moment, peered inside and helped herself, but she was not greedy. She showed what she had taken.

'That doesn't seem enough to me, old mother!' Aethelstan said in a low voice.

'It will do, sire!' she said, for the very first time acknowledging his status and title.

He bowed his head in acquiescence to her and Judith then turned his horse and walked back to his witan. Ceorl looked at him with hopeful sheep's eyes and a silent question.

'She will write, but give her time. Don't hound her!' Aethelstan advised. 'Now, witan! We are to march on Constantine's stronghold and see what we have to do there. Olaf may have done me a big favour by bolting. Gossip always spreads with the eagle's wings. Other kings may be impressed enough to seek me out, but first Constantine. We march when the men are ready. Not before.'

'Any specific plans, sire?' Cerdic asked.

Aethelstan shook his head. 'We'll get there first and see what this fortress looks like!' and

100

he paused a minute. 'I'll not send brave men to their deaths for a hopeless situation!'

The witan exchanged nods. This king was no butcher. Rannulf stood and listened to every word. He was not part of the witan, considered far too young, but they permitted his presence as he was a scribe with a growing reputation.

A week later Aethelstan reflected as he stared ahead. Before him was a natural, monstrous fortification, just about impregnable. With dark clouds of evening hovering overhead, it seemed to menace the king and his army, making them almost puny. He sat for a while studying the general layout plus the land available on either side. It became obvious there was only one thing to do, but he could imagine the protests from his witan.

'That's going to be a nasty one to take!' Egbert commented thoughtfully, and Oswald, Cerdic and Ceorl nodded while Rannulf stared with amazement at this incredible fortification. He realised his experience of life was limited but never in his wildest nightmares had he envisaged something like this. He eyed his king with interest and waited like the rest of them.

'Siege, sire?' Oswald asked trying to work out the best tactics.

Aethelstan shook his head firmly. 'That would take too long and there's no telling what mischief might be started elsewhere in England in my absence. Get some men to go out hunting and kill a top-quality stag or two!!'

The king grinned at their bewilderment. 'I'll explain later. What I plan to do is this. Ride out, on my own, and see if Constantine has the balls to do the same and face me, man to man!'

'What!' his gesith chorused in total horror! 'Out of the question, sire!' Cerdic said for all of them. 'Doesn't make sense at all. Risking your life . . .' and words left him with shock at the very idea.

'No! Hear me out!' Aethelstan explained quickly. 'There can be two gesith members nearby but I must go alone. That puts Constantine in a very bad position with his own men if he doesn't copy me. See?'

Slowly they did, if unhappy with the idea in general. 'But the dead stags?'

'Bribery and corruption for his followers. They'll only have so much food in that place,' and he nodded ahead. 'They'll be delighted with fresh meat and happy with it too. It will also impress them I have the men and time to send them out hunting!'

Cerdic chewed it over and had to admit it held merit, though it was anathema to all of them for their king to go forward unguarded.

'Trust me, witan!'

They knew they had little choice but were unhappy. After all, he was—their king.

Aethelstan read them easily. 'I shall want the very best horse. Able to respond swiftly if the need arises, but also quiet enough to stand for a while so he must be well fed first. I don't want a horse snatching at his bit to graze. I shall wear my very best royal clothes to make an impression.'

The next morning even the witan had to approve, though still uneasy. They had managed to persuade their king to let two gesith riders be at his rear while he went forward alone. Aethelstan dressed with extreme care after washing thoroughly. Next to his skin he wore a gay coloured silk shirt, and his tunic was such a slashing combination of scarlet and bright blue it was almost flamboyant. His short trousers were also bright blue and his cross garters scarlet. He was bare-headed and on a chestnut stallion, very well fed indeed. His posture shouted he was royal and dominant.

Cerdic would have been happier if he had worn chain mail under the top tunic, but he did not suggest this, knowing full well the idea would be instantly negated. He made sure the rest of the gesith were on high alert and also had a quiet word with Burhred. There was something about the harsh, grizzled mercenary that appealed to him.

'Lose many men?' he asked late that previous evening.

'Four dead, two will die. The women will help them along. Nothing can be done for them. Battleaxe wounds,' he explained bluntly.

They both knew the lethal destruction caused by a well-aimed battleaxe with muscles behind the blow. 'Down to just a handful of us now, Lord.'

'Are you happy with your oaths here or do you intend to offer them elsewhere?' was Cerdic's next pointed question.

Burhred shook his head firmly. 'We are happy to stay here. Our pickings have been very profitable,' and he gave a wolfish grin. The witan impressed him with the way they worked together as a polished team.

'Families?'

Burhred shook his head. 'None of us have any, Lord, that's why we banded together in the first place with the bishop, God rest his soul.'

'You are Christians?'

'We are indeed, Lord!'

'Good,' Cerdic grunted. 'This witan is always ready to acknowledge top-quality fighters,' he explained and gave Burhred a knowing look, which was a silent promise that if he behaved well there might be promotion to the gesith in due course. They both understood each other, two hard-bitten experienced warriors, even if one was well into middle age. A rapport flowed between them that both recognised.

They all studied their king as he mounted his horse. Every man impressed with the magnificent picture he cut, Aethelstan grinned down at them. 'Now let's see if Constantine has any balls at all!' he chuckled.

He rode forward at a walk with two gesith members at his rear. Then he halted, turned, and with his right hand indicated they were to follow him no more. They did not like this, neither did the witan, but their king seemed to know what he was doing.

His horse walked forward again then stopped as Aethelstan sat quietly waiting. He was enormously amused by the situation in general. Ahead stretched the gloomy fortress with no sign of life, but he could feel many eyes on him, wondering, waiting and calculating. Was he bait for some kind of trap? If no trap and Constantine failed to appear, it would mean he had ignored Aethelstan's challenge. He would be scorned and damned for all time for cowardice and all his men would know. He would be shamed before them all.

After a seemingly long wait, movement appeared ahead—one man on a horse with two guards at his back. This thicker, older man also gestured and halted his guards then warily rode forward. Olaf had called Aethelstan a devil king yet here facing him was a most handsome, confident young man dressed magnificently. There was a pleasant smile of welcome on his face, which further disconcerted Constantine.

'Well met, brother king!' Aethelstan greeted him cheerily.

Constantine was momentarily lost for

words. 'What's your game?' he growled at last.

'Game? Is there one? Do tell me!' Aethelstan riposted with another flashing smile, illuminating his splendid face and fair hair.

'What do you want?' Constantine almost spat out with his temper rising. He was being made a fool of and it stuck in his proud throat.

'Just a chat between us,' Aethelstan said gently, having weighed up the other's mood in a flash. 'I think there has been far too much trouble for too many years between our peoples. Surely in these modern times we should be able to discuss a situation?'

Constantine could not think of a sufficiently cutting retort while, at the same time, he had to agree a point had been made. He was well informed from his spies and knew the land and power held by Aethelstan, as well as all the ships he was having constructed in the southeast of the island. Did he plan a future invasion? When and why?

'What do you have in mind?' he asked warily.

'I am the king of this new England. Will you acknowledge me as such?' and though it was a gentle question Constantine did not miss the barb at its ending.

'You mean, be Under King to you?' he barked.

'Am I such an ogre?'

'That would stick in my throat!' Constantine

106

managed to get out at last.

'We both know there can only be one senior overall king and surely it is he with the largest territory and army, wouldn't you say?' Aethelstan paused to add with heavy meaning: 'It would mean many men's lives could be saved.'

Constantine knew he heard the truth. Men could die in their hundreds because of what he said or did now.

'I don't like it,' he grumbled.

Aethelstan scented victory. 'There is much in my past life I abhorred, but I could do nothing about it then. I simply had to suffer and bide my time. It was very hard often but I can never be held responsible for throwing men into battle to suffer and die unnecessarily. My conscience is very clear indeed, brother king.'

Constantine seethed inside. He stared hard at this young handsome god who sat on his horse, totally relaxed, reins in his left hand. His right hand rested casually on his right thigh, though he could see it would have only a small distance to travel to reach the hilt of the most magnificent sword he had ever seen. The younger man's gaze was steady and stonily probing. For a short crazy handful of breaths, it had entered Constantine's head to charge forward and kill Aethelstan of England—then he knew it would be him who would die. They were meeting, not under any banner of truce,

107

so an attack as such would not be against understood rules, but his sense told him he would be the one to die. He also realised, with a shock, that Aethelstan had read his mind because now his stare had turned sardonic, even scornful.

'Very well,' he said sourly at last.

'Excellent, brother king. We can meet in a week's time at Penrith. I expect to have visits from others as well.'

Constantine went on high alert. 'Who?'

Aethelstan gave a false nonchalant shrug. It had been a near thing. 'Stupid man!" he told himself. 'I'll introduce you then,' he added airily. 'I have two excellent scribes with me and they can draw up our Charter of Penrith!'

Constantine knew he was beaten. If he could only keep breathing long enough there would have to be some event of reckoning in the future. Here and now was neither the time nor the place. Also he had enough nous to know he could never do such alone when Aethelstan could call up fighting men from the whole of the country. He let out his breath in a deep, heavy sigh.

'Penrith in a week!' and he swung his horse around to trot back to his two gesith guards. At the same time, Aethelstan half turned and nodded to his two men who cantered up to place themselves one at the front and the other to his rear. They carefully escorted their king back to his agitated witan where he dismounted and gladly took a beaker of ale.

'Well, it went like this, though at one point the fool did think about trying to take me out!' and he chuckled. His witan did not. They exchanged looks of horror. This would never be allowed to happen again. They listened with care. 'I think today's events will spread like wildfire,' Aethelstan told them. 'Once this has all been dealt with we go to Pucklechurch to welcome our continental guests. You men with families are to go home and see them. There are still other parts of the kingdom I'll have to visit, including back to York again to check my mint is producing *my* money, not Danish coins. I have decided there will be 240 silver pennies to make a pound. The coins can be made capable of being split for smaller amounts for traders, but *my* coinage it will be,' he stated firmly. 'And I intend to call a grand council in the southeast when I get time. I also want an up-to-date report on the building of my ships. My bones tell me one day I'll have to sail up to Scotland for some reason, so I wish to be prepared at all times. I hope you scribes are getting all this down, and remember, I welcome all scholars to my court from any country and race.'

Rannulf continued scribbling fast, blessing Ceorl's hint about learning shortcuts for words to make speed. He puffed out his cheeks and quickly scanned what he had written. He could get all that back and saw he was just ahead of Ceorl. They were going to have much best writing to do and a charter was something he had not yet attempted. Then he could go home to see his Osburga. There would be so much to tell her.

Ceorl finally ended and smiled at Rannulf's almost smug grin at having finished first, then he saw a courier dismounting and coming directly to him, a sealed note in his hand. He took it while his heart gave a wild flutter of hope. Had she sent him a letter? Where was she now?

Aethelstan did not miss this as colour flared in Ceorl's cheeks. 'Clear off, scribe, and read your letter in privacy!' he said with amusement and kindness. Ceorl bolted to be alone. 'It seemed old love was worse than young love!' Aethelstan told himself with amusement. He caught Cerdic's eye and they grinned openly at each other.

Aethelstan gave a sniff. 'Do I smell roast venison?'

'Yes, sir. Two stags so busy fighting each other over the hinds we were able to take both out. The ladies will have to go elsewhere!' Oswald informed him.

'Right. Get some men to take them over to where I met Constantine,' and Aethelstan held up a wet finger. 'The breeze is from us to them. They'll smell our dinner all right. Leave the stags where they are easily collected. Even if Constantine does not like me you can bet his men will. They're bound to be short of fresh meat. Another sore in their sub-king's wounds!!' he chuckled.

A group of warriors also saw the joke and hastened to sling the dead stag on long shoulder poles and carry, then drop the carcass where their king had stood. Even as they began to withdraw men came from the other side, intent on having their own roast venison for their meal.

Ceorl explained carefully. 'A charter or treaty is a very formal document, which will be read and examined by many, so there will be some decorative work to be added. I'll go into that tomorrow. Right now I have my own private letter to write, so clear off somewhere.'

Rannulf smothered a grin. He knew Ceorl had read the short letter a number of times already and obviously wanted to pour out his heart to his Judith. Even though their courier system was good, medicine women did not stay in one place for long at all. He felt sympathy for his father. When could he expect another letter? Especially as they were moving back home after this important meeting at Penrith, and the king was talking about going to so many places of his realm. At least his own love life could proceed along gentler paths. If there should be a bishop at Pucklechurch he and Osburga could marry properly. He itched to talk it all over with her.

Aethelstan drew Cerdic to one side as he

took another of what he called his thinking walks. 'What is your opinion of Burhred the mercenary?'

'I like him, sire. He's a tough no-nonsense man. I'm glad he's on our side and not against us!'

'In that case I want a word with him. You stay as witness!' and Aethelstan looked around, spotted Burhred and pointed him out to Cerdic.

With a gesture Burhred came striding over. Worried. Kings did not speak to the likes of mercenaries without good reason, so what had he done to offend?

'Do you know anything about the sea?' Aethelstan asked shortly.

Burhred blinked at such an unexpected question. 'A little, sire,' he replied cautiously.

'Do you get seasick?'

Cerdic was as puzzled as Burhred. Now what was their king planning? Rack his brains as he might he failed to produce a logical answer.

'No, sire. As it happens I've been out in rough times when many were sick but not me!'

Aethelstan nodded with satisfaction and looked at Cerdic whom he could see was baffled. He strolled on a few more paces then turned to face his two men squarely.

'I don't trust Constantine. He will cede to me now because I'm bigger and stronger but I'm looking ahead. I want a sea force, a navy that can sail up the coast as far as Caithness if necessary. I can't run a land as well as a sea campaign. I want a reliable man to conduct the latter for me. Are you literate?'

Burhred pulled a bit of a face. 'I can read and write but not too well, sire,' he said honestly. 'Lack of practice, I suppose. Mercenaries like me don't have a great need for writing.'

Both Aethelstan and Cerdic understood this logic and now Cerdic saw the king's plan. How farsighted and shrewd.

'Well, do you want the job of commanding my fleet, because if so you'll have to brush up on your writing, as I'll want written reports and observations at all times,' Aethelstan said.

Burhred blinked and nodded hard. 'I'd very much like such a job, sire!'

'Good! It's yours. Liaise with my witan after I've spoken to them, and while we ride to Penrith get busy improving your reading and writing. Young Rannulf will tutor you because his father is going to be far too busy. I have no time for verbal reports. A message starts off saying something but when it's been through half a dozen messengers it can end up being delivered as the opposite of what it was.'

Burhred nodded and walked away considerably bemused. This was something he had never envisaged and he was flattered and proud at his selection. He also approved of the project as a whole. This was indeed a very farsighted king.

The witan were also filled with admiration, because such a sea campaign had never crossed their minds, yet they all knew the Great King Alfred had believed in such, though the times then were not right.

Rannulf was amazed at this new task but bent to it with his usual personal enthusiasm. Initially he had been wary of this hard-bitten mercenary, but Burhred was keen and after a short while they settled down together working as a team. Ceorl was thankful. He had much royal work to do as well as his long letter to Judith, in which he had poured out his heart. He wanted to hear from her again but was realistic enough to know this could take many long weeks. First of all she had to be found— she could be anywhere. Only numerous enquiries by word of mouth would locate her, by which time he could well be back in Mercia. He yearned to discuss all this with someone but Rannulf was not that person and Cerdic seemed to be spending so much time with the king as well as their witan meetings. With gloom he knew he could only wait and hope.

SEVEN

Aethelstan did not go to Penrith with all of his army. He left enough fighters to keep his peace yet still managed to move with enough men to impress. When he did arrive he was pleased to greet other sub-kings, who were most willing to join with him: Eldred I of Bamburgh as well as Constantine and Owen of Strathclyde, then Hywel Dda of Deheubarth, and Owain of Glywysing and Gwent joined in, all prepared to sign the Treaty of Penrith, accepting him as King of England. It was hinted to him that in due course, obviously after reflection, King Tewdr of Brycheiniog would also be happy to join in. There was much discussion amid feasting and ale-drinking, but Aethelstan kept his wits about him. He agreed with the Welsh kings that the boundary would be the River Wye. He remained conscious there were still some small minor kings in other parts of Wales who might require a fight, but the allies he now had were tremendous. He invited them all to attend his royal court as and when they wished and there was a good atmosphere when even Constantine began to unbend.

The witan gathered informally. 'We have seen history made here,' Cerdic commented thoughtfully. 'I never thought to live to see this day!'

'Great King Alfred would be so delighted and proud of his grandson!' Ceorl said to the other three.

'Will it last though?' Egbert questioned soberly. 'Where is Anlaf?'

'Rumour has it he's at Dublin!' Oswald replied. 'With Guthfrithson, and he has Norse warriors.'

Cerdic chewed this over. 'I still think our king could muster the greatest army if needed with his new allies, especially as he will have a navy!'

This was a most important point. 'I understand he wishes to call a great council at Colchester after he's been down to Exeter, then he plans to go back to York again,' Ceorl said heavily. 'All this riding and travelling is getting hard work for me. Our king is young and energetic. I'm not anymore. I often find it agony to dismount from the saddle. In short I suppose I'm just getting too old.'

'I know what you mean,' Cerdic agreed. 'I've lost my love affair with the saddle too. I suppose what it boils down to is the fact this witan has become a stay-at-home, though who would advise the king on his journeys? It's going to become a great problem. I'll have to have a private word with him.'

'Rannulf is more than capable now of travelling as his scribe,' Ceorl confirmed. 'I took him on and trained him at just the right time.'

116

It was not until the next day that Cerdic was able to get the king alone and relate their discussion. 'We have grown too old, sire.'

Aethelstan was startled enough to be quite taken aback. Like all young people he could not envisage age and he knew he would miss these two wise elders desperately.

'How abut some kind of cart?' he asked hopefully.

Cerdic pulled a face and cringed at the very idea. 'All those bumps over tracks with our old joints, sire?'

'I can't do without you!' Aethelstan said flatly. 'I'll have to think of something. I must have my witan even if I don't always agree with your opinions, especially you and Ceorl.'

'Rannulf is very good now, sire. Ceorl swears by him!'

This was an unexpected problem for Aethelstan, especially when he remembered back to his wondrous aunt and how she always rode forth and led her men into battle. Were females tougher than they appeared? It was a new and interesting thought. He knew about the agonies of childbirth, which females bore with incredible fortitude, so was it this that made them so rugged and stoical? Were men's superior muscles nothing but some kind of façade?

'I know where I intend to go. How about you four men of my witan riding on ahead at your leisure, with an appropriate guard and

117

escort of course? At least you'd be in my area. Once my England firmly settles down it will be so much simpler. Please?' and he gave Cerdic the full blast of his natural charm.

Cerdic capitulated. 'Well, we can try it, sire. We could do with the magic joint potions of a medicine woman to help our knees at least!'

'That is it then!' Aethelstan cried. 'Where are they? Get scouts out to find them for me! Hurry! This is vital! Bring them here without delay!'

It was later that Ceorl came up with the idea they jointly presented to the king.

'Sire, there is also another solution. You should have witans elsewhere who could all meet for a grand conference. Take London for example. You could do with people keeping an eye on the tolls of ships and trade goods coming in for your treasury. The same with York. Another in that city. We could be your witan in our home territory.'

Aethelstan blinked. Why hadn't he considered that? 'What about writing?'

'A young scribe is what you need. Not an oldie like me. Reports could reach me at an agreed home base and I could collate them for your scrutiny, as and when.'

'That is an idea. Let me ponder a little. I do have some good men at London but they're not official, though I believe they're trustworthy and not robbing me. They do have a scribe!' and he nodded. That would sort out this problem once and for all, but how he would miss talking to this particular group of four men. They had become nothing but cherished and favourite uncles to him, because a king's could be a very lonely occupation. 'In the interim let's see if the old medicine woman can help, bring her here!'

He walked off by himself, deep in complicated thought. Grandfather King Alfred had always set great store by London's trading. The once empty spaces between Queenshythe and Billingsgate were filled with new wharves into which traders welcomed ships carrying everything from wine to cloths. There was a rich revenue in tolls available to him as king, and he had to admit, he had become so obsessed with Northumbria he had allowed this to go to the back of his mind. He rebuked himself soundly because York would be growing and booming as another centre of trade. He did indeed need excellent men in these places. It was unrealistic to expect his personal witan to be everywhere. As long as he had regular written reports, so much could be dealt with in the homes of Cerdic and Ceorl. If Rannulf planned to marry shortly there was a chance his wife would object to him being away so much, whereas work at home for him would be highly acceptable. He made his decision: groups of counsellors elsewhere, who would liaise with him and each other in writing. He walked back to his four men to explain his thinking, but he would still have the old mother here to aid their health. They were indeed getting old and, once again, he berated himself for his lack of foresight.

*   *   *

Judith read her letter yet again and was confused. How could someone talk with the quill and make such flowing sentences? She examined the writing material. It was made from a very fine animal's skin with another joined at the end to make quite a large roll. She became aware of the old mother's eyes upon her with a peculiar smile.

'He appears to love you very much,' she commented.

Judith gave a shake of her head. 'I just don't know what to think about it all,' she replied frankly. 'I'm quite content travelling around with you, sleeping and hunting for ourselves,' she admitted.

'Those days are coming to an end,' the older woman said unexpectedly. 'I am exceedingly old and I feel in myself my time is not far off. You'll wake up one morning and I'll have gone,' she said bluntly.

Judith was shocked. 'No!' she protested.

'Yes!' was her reply. 'I have seen sixty-five summers.'

'I'd no idea you were so old!'

'Well I am, and I'm not prepared to go

120

through another winter. Now is your chance to make a fresh life for yourself. Take it!'

Judith felt tears hover. Although not related, she looked upon the old woman as kinfolk. 'I've followed you for a number of years now.'

'And it's high time you moved on! You have a first-class knowledge of making medicines from plants, rendering down animal fats, mixing the correct herbs in them. I've shown you how to make the killing drink to put a warrior out of his misery. I have nothing left to teach you and you have the opportunity to make a fresh start in life. Take it while it is there!'

Judith wept openly. She knew the old woman had a will of iron and she would wake up in her little tent to find herself alone. 'I'll think about it all,' she prevaricated slowly.

It was the next morning her hand was forced when a weary scout appeared. 'Found you at last!'

The old woman gave him a penetrating stare. 'The king has some kind of problem with two men of his witan and he begs help!'

'Where is he?' the old woman wanted to know, though she had a good idea of that and what had happened at Penrith. Any traveller could be questioned because all had the highest respect for obvious medicine women. Information became simple to acquire and when coupled with shrewd knowledge of a person's character, conclusions were not hard to find. This king was young, dynamic and unstoppable. He was filled with the blood of the Great King Alfred and the remarkable Lady of Mercia. This was a heaven-sent opportunity and she turned to her upset acolyte. 'You'll go with him. Not me,' she pronounced in a tone that brooked no argument.

Judith looked at her aghast. 'But that means he'll be there. I'm not ready for him!' she protested.

'You'll still go, girl! Bring an extra horse in the morning. There's a vil not far away,' she ordered brusquely to the warrior. He had no intention of getting into an argument with a healing woman. He'd only come off worse, but he was puzzled by the sudden distress on the face of the younger female. What was the mysterious situation here?

Judith's world had begun to collapse around her and she sat crying freely with bowed head. As the warrior rode away the older woman rested one hand, crippled with joint ills, in her fingers, and squeezed. 'Make your new life. Remember our years together but allow me to vanish to make my own destiny. Just remember all I've taught you. The plants and herbs to use for the various situations and the exact proportions to make the drink to ease the dying warrior from his misery. Wherever you wander study the plant life around you and collect those to be needed. Dry them or brew them. Always have a pouch with you for this purpose and a very sharp knife as well as flints to make fire. Be careful that the water you drink is pure at all times. As to men, use your common sense and follow your instincts. We part now.'

Judith understood. In the morning the old mother would have gone—where? She knew she would never be able to stay awake. They often walked so far by evening her legs were exhausted. She looked up at the old face and controlled her tears at last.

'I'll miss you so much,' she whispered throatily.

The old woman felt the same but refrained from further comment. She gave another squeeze to the younger woman's shoulder and firmly turned away. She would pack what was necessary and in the middle of the night steal off. She too felt a lump in her throat, but the parting was inevitable and age controlled her. Nothing bad lasted forever; neither did anything good. Life was a pure balancing act and hers had been good and fascinating. She was going to do only what had happened to her so many years ago, back in the distant mists of time and memories.

Judith woke just as the dawn chorus started, remembered with a start and bolted from her little tent. She stood miserably. Quite alone. This was something she had never experienced in her thirty years of life and she felt naked and vulnerable. Always before there had been someone around. Even a person she disliked would be better than this. She hastily pulled on tunic and trousers, then realised her stomach was empty. There was a little pottage left in the container and she hastily wolfed it down and kept looking around for human life. Even a wild animal would have been better company than this unaccustomed solitude. They too had vanished, so she sank to squat on her heels and wallow in some deep self-pity.

She heard the approaching horses first and brightened as the warrior returned, riding one and leading another. He scanned the area, then turned to study the girl's wan face, but he noted how her eyes brightened as he dismounted and strolled over holding both sets of reins attached to the snaffle bits.

'So,' he said slowly, with sudden, sharp understanding, 'the old mother has moved on then?' He had heard tales of how they could vanish when it suited them for their personal reasons. Did this situation mean he was going to have trouble with this young one?

Judith could manage only a nod as she stood and collected her plant pouch and her folded small tent. He hastily took charge, aware he was under direct command from his king. The tent was strapped to his horse's flank, then he helped his passenger mount, eyeing her seat critically.

'Do we have far to go?' Judith asked him. She was more used to walking than riding and she had grave reservations about her abilities with this form of transport. She felt a heavy weight in her heart but forced an artificial, bland look on her face.

'The king is now heading for his palace at Pucklechurch, which is well over a hundred miles away. We may catch him up, we may not. Depends upon the pace he sets,' the warrior explained—and this girl's riding ability.

'I'm not used to horses!' Judith told him in a worried tone.

'Relax, lady. I'll take it easy for you. Would also be quite a change for me too!' and he grinned affably over at her as their horses walked off side by side. Was she one of these talkative females? He hoped not because small talk had never been his line of activity.

He moved them into a trot, which Judith hated. 'Canter!' she called. At least it would be more comfortable. 'How long before we can catch up?'

He considered. 'Might be tomorrow. We'll stay tonight. Reeves have been warned in advance to feed and provide a chamber as we're on the king's business.'

'For what?' was her next question.

He pulled a face and gave a whimsical shrug. 'Not my place to question kings, lady!'

Judith saw his point, though was puzzled. Did he expect a battle in this direction? If so,

125

from whom? Like the old mother she had a shrewd idea of the political situation, because everyone talked freely to a valued medicine female.

They reached shelter by early evening, just as Judith knew she could not stay in the saddle any longer. She fell from it and leaned heavily on the saddle flaps.

'I want another mount tomorrow,' she said firmly. 'This animal is uncomfortable. Back too long, shoulders too straight. Poor paces.'

He was taken aback and knew she was right but had simply taken the first available spare mount. 'You know something about horses, lady?'

'Enough!' was all she could manage. She wanted a hot meal and drink. Most of all a hot wash and clean clothes, then she had to sort out in her mind about the scribe. How should she handle him? The old mother's words were so clear and made sense but was she ready for a second marriage? Her first had been a disaster and she had simply walked away from a grumpy husband with selfish ideas. She'd heard later on he had been killed in a feud fight, so she was eligible as single. But she knew she felt nothing for him. Then she rebuked herself. 'Be fair. You've not had time to get to know him. Give him a chance!"

Her horse the next day had been more carefully selected and certainly gave a smoother ride, but muscles unused to this

126

transport pulled with pain as they stretched. She had taken the precaution to rub into her knees some special cream, which she made herself and this helped a little.

The next day she was starting to despair when he stood in his stirrups and pointed ahead. 'That's the tail end. Come! Canter on!' he encouraged.

It was Cerdic who first spotted two riders threading their way through to the front. Ceorl turned, gasped and went scarlet.

'Don't!' Cerdic warned. 'It's the king who has sent for her for our knees. She must go to him before us!'

Ceorl almost exploded but did as he was told, though could not refrain from throwing a beaming smile at her as she rode past.

Aethelstan was also surprised at her sudden appearance. 'The old mother?' he asked pulling his horse to walk it alongside hers.

'Gone, sire!'

'Gone! Gone? What do you mean?'

Judith brought him up to date. 'It's the way it happens, sire. The very old always know and just disappear in the middle of the night, but she had forewarned me. She also said there was nothing left for her to teach me. I just go on my own path now.'

Aethelstan realised he was totally ignorant of the lives of medicine ladies, because they made a point of keeping themselves to themselves. Now the young one had turned up and from his eye corner he could see his senior scribe staring hard, almost quivering, with his need for speech.

'I'm heading down for my palace at Pucklechurch for a special meeting, but two of my oldsters have homes on the way. They'll break off to go there. You'd better go with them and all join me later,' he said not unkindly. How much did she really know about healing matters?

Judith gave a nod then turned her horse aside and instantly Ceorl appeared.

'Judith! This has made my day. Did you get my letter?'

'Yes, thank you.'

Ceorl hesitated with his words. 'I know I don't cut much of a figure compared to a warrior but my heart is yours. Please let us get to know each other!' he begged, then paused to sort out the next words. 'The king will be at Pucklechurch and there'll be a bishop there. I think my son will arrange to marry his betrothed.'

Judith gave him a stern look. 'So?'

Ceorl plunged. 'Would you think of marrying me at the same time? We'll be going to my home for a couple of nights so you can see how I live. You'll never want. That I vow. It might be months again before a bishop becomes available. Please?'

Judith's instinct was to give a flat 'No!' then she reflected. Church bishops did not grow on trees and she had a suspicion there was no nearby monastery. The old mother's words reverberated in her head.

'I will think for a few days,' she managed to get out at last.

Ceorl clasped her right hand in his left, squeezed it, then had the sense to turn back to his riding place and not push himself forward anymore. Cerdic threw him a silent question and he whispered what had been said.

'Let it go at that,' Cerdic advised his pal. 'Don't press any harder. It's the lady's prerogative to make the decision, not yours,' he advised.

'I'm going to die a thousand deaths until she speaks,' he hissed back.

'Tough!' was Cerdic's response but his eyes twinkled. This was far worse than Rannulf and Osburga. He would have so much to tell his joy and every hoof beat was taking him nearer. He bubbled internally with his own excitement as they came to their home territory, and this rose until Cerdic was cantering. He half fell from his saddle as Edith rushed up. He grabbed her in his usual bear hug, showering kisses upon her. 'My joy!' was all he could manage. Then Rannulf vaulted from his horse and treated a wildly excited Osburga in the same way. Ceorl and Judith watched, Ceorl with envy, Judith with astonishment.

'That's true love,' Ceorl murmured.

Judith stared with more amazement at two

magnificent homes. 'Who do these belong to?' she asked with awe.

'The larger one is Cerdic and Edith's. The other is mine.'

'But who lives with you?'

'My son Rannulf, but once he is married he'll build his own home nearby. We are going to end up a vil in our own right.'

Judith was speechless and highly impressed. She had never envisaged such magnificence and she shook her head with bewilderment. And this small man was ready to share this with her? For the first time she felt humbled.

'Come, let me show you around,' Ceorl said as she dismounted and as men came up to take their mounts away. 'Freed slaves of gebur status. They are willing and totally loyal. They have given their oaths to me as their Lord.'

'I'd no idea!' Judith managed to get out at last.

'The two of us are earldormen, don't forget,' he reminded her gently. 'We must show we live up to our status,' he joked gently and took her inside.

She had a sharp memory of life in a tiny tent, especially in the cold months. From that—to this? Old mother was right as usual. All this could be hers. Inside it was still not fully furnished or decorated, because furniture was yet to be made, but it was comfortable and the weapons on the walls, set in a decorative pattern, fascinated her, as did the stone floor, thickly spread with fresh, sweet-smelling rushes. It was a commodious, welcoming home, the likes of which she had never encountered before. She became aware he was watching her closely, even anxiously, and she turned to him. 'I think it is all quite splendid, Earldorman Ceorl!'

He wanted to speak but did not quite dare, Cerdic was right. He must be patient, but how his heart screamed for her. If only she would consent to a double wedding. He controlled his tongue and said not a word but gently walked her around, displaying every feature.

Judith took it all in. There would be comfort here the like of which she had never known, then she thought about the medicine skills inculcated into her by the old mother. Were they to be wasted? It made a thorny problem. She knew there were others like her, though the old mother had never mixed and neither did those others. Each recognised another's skill and calling with respect, but it was rare for them even to exchange a word. They were not unlike wandering churls, sticking to their individual paths and destinies. How would she feel after a time living in a house, no matter how splendid? She might miss the free wandering. Her heart and mind became confused. At least here there were other females, so she would not be friendless in that way, but—and she wavered with uncertainty.

'Did I mention we are all going down to the

king's court at Pucklechurch and that includes Edith and Osburga,' he told her. Why didn't she say something? 'The king hopes you can help with the knee problems for riding,' he carried on, worried at her silence. 'Can you?'

'I expect I can mix something up for both of you to be put on the knees, but the cream will have to work in slowly. That means some kind of long dressing to be wound about the knee. Like an animal skin, cut narrow and joined to make a long roll,' she explained, glad to get back on ground that was safer to her. 'I'd want animal fat rendering down then I'll mix in herbs, so when it cools it becomes easy to rub in the knee joints.'

Now it was his turn to pay attention to her words. 'The king is going to make more panels of advisers all over the island, so hopefully long-distance riding will diminish.'

She nodded at that. This made sense. Middle-aged men like him were beyond hours and days in the saddle. After her ride here, even though fairly short, she understood the problem. How her own knees ached.

'Come and meet Edith and Osburga. You'll like them,' he said, and turning led her outside. She still had given him no hint and he racked his brains as to what he could next do.

*   *   *

Aethelstan sat his horse and looked ahead

132

and down at the mighty River Severn from the exact spot he had sat with his aunt all those years ago. So much had happened since then it was remarkable to think he now had the England that Grandfather Alfred and dear Aunt Aethelflaeda had struggled to obtain. It was his England, though he was realistic enough to admit that there were still rocky parts. The treaty signed at Penrith was invaluable and seemed to be holding. The fact other kings had signed as well as Constantine was a bonus to him. So now he must bring the other sub-kings into this English fold to further consolidate his position.

He let his mind wander to London as well as York, the great trading centres that brought in so much good revenue to his treasury. With advisers in other parts, liaising one with the other as well as himself, he felt even more secure. How he would miss his current witan, yet he was honest enough to acknowledge that what he saw as decent riding was sheer hard labour to older men. Even with a medicine woman present it was unlikely her skills could rejuvenate older men.

His mind turned to this palace. It had never been a very good one, unlike others at Tamworth and Stafford, yet it was conveniently placed for him to take men and ride down to Exeter and deal with the far southwest Celts. Always known as a difficult lot. Part of this palace could be called dilapidated, but it must suffice with representatives from continental noble families coming to meet his sisters with a view to matrimony. Agents had already arrived with many superb gifts, as his passion for collecting books and relics was well known. Students were also coming from various countries to sojourn at his court for intellectual discussions. Once he had been to Exeter he could ride back to a more commodious palace.

He turned and trotted back to the palace, seeing it with fresh eyes. It really was rundown, but he had to go in, to greet his continental visitors, as he now spotted a small party approaching. He waited and beamed his enormous, genuine pleasure as Cerdic, Edith, Rannulf, Osburga and Ceorl with his Judith all dismounted and came up to him.

'Good lady wife. Your appearance warms my eyes!' Aethelstan told her and it was no false flattery. He did so much admire her and possibly if he could have met her like, he would have discounted his vow to refuse matrimony and produce an heir. Edith was rare and he suspected her daughter came from the same mould. About this Judith he was uncertain, though he respected the talents she would obviously have. He threw a swift look at his scribe who stood rather self-consciously alongside the medicine woman. Perhaps this was going to be a failed relationship? If so what about this work? There were so many messages now to go forth for everyone to understand his precise wishes. Although Rannulf had become so skilled there was far too much writing for him alone. He might now lose Ceorl.

He cleared his throat and nodded at his scribe. 'A private word with you, the rest of you go in, find appropriate chambers for yourselves. I'll join you shortly,' he told them graciously, and they took his broad hint. Osburga took Judith by one hand, grinned at her and, leaving Rannulf in their wake, led the way in what she thought was the correct direction.

Aethelstan turned to Ceorl. 'How fare matters, scribe?'

Ceorl gave him a solemn look and shrugged. 'She won't say yes and she won't say no, sire,' he replied miserably. 'I don't know what to do. Cerdic says be patient but I had prayed for a wedding here like Rannulf and Osburga.'

Aethelstan gave a deep sigh. This would not do at all when he had letters to write that would keep both scribes working for hours. 'Send her out to me here but I don't promise anything!' he added hastily, seeing hope spark in his scribe's eyes. 'Get her now!'

Judith came soon, wondering what this was about. 'Walk with me, will you,' Aethelstan said gently. 'I have a problem. Perhaps you can advise?'

Judith blinked. How could she advise a crowned king of England? Her instincts as a

135

medicine woman rose high. 'Are you sickening, sire?'

Aethelstan nodded, keeping a very straight face. 'It's not of the body but the heart and mind,' he told her frankly, turning and facing her, 'and you are my only hope,' he began carefully. He had worked it out that any medicine woman would have a natural still tongue. It would be part and parcel of their calling, which was shrouded in total secrecy at all times. Taking his time, he outlined his regal plans, his other witans and advisers and the vast distances of land to cover to keep control of his England, which was not yet stable, the Treaty of Penrith notwithstanding. 'My scribes are of critical importance to me. I just don't know how I'll manage if my senior man is lovesick!'

It struck Judith as amusing and she laughed gaily, her whole serious face lighting up. 'I'm not used to talking to kings, sire,' she began. 'I'm only used to the old mother and warriors in enormous pain. I appreciate your frankness and your open comments will stay just with me. That I promise. Now it's my turn. I've seen the scribe's home. I am awfully impressed but also worried. How would I fit in? I'm used to roaming and a little tent. The transition is so great and . . .' She halted to shake her head dubiously. 'What if I became bored and restless to be roaming again? It could happen. I simply do not know!'

Aethelstan could see her point, which was honestly valid. He thought furiously. 'How about a compromise?' he began delicately, and she frowned, not understanding. 'Tell him you want breathing space, because travelling has been the only life you've known, and stay with Cerdic's wife. You could see Ceorl on a regular basis. Let him court you in the old-fashioned way. Both of you take your time for, say, a year?'

'What a splendid idea, sire! That's the perfect solution! I'll go and tell him right now. King Aethelstan, I think you're one very smart king!'

With a respectful bow of her head she turned and hurried to Ceorl, who stood to one side, wondering what exactly was going on.

Aethelstan gave a sigh of relief. Another problem solved. Now for his lovely sisters and noble visitors.

EIGHT

Aethelstan felt supremely satisfied with life in general. His half sisters had been greatly admired and showered with gifts from continental noble families of Francia and Germany, as well as Duke Hugh. They would be well set up for life but, more important to him, was the knowledge he could always call on these new brothers-in-law for extra men at arms if needed. It was critically important to follow Grandfather Alfred's example with continental connections.

He had made it clear any son could attend his court for training and fostering, and once they appeared and this happened it would even further strengthen his continental links. There had been a generous exchange of gifts with relics and wonderful books, which he had seen distributed to the church and monasteries. At the same time, there had been many enquiries for scholars to come to his court to study and learn, all of which he endorsed wholeheartedly.

He had ridden down to Exeter, but, although there was a rough-and-ready skirmish, no actual battle had developed. Instead he had sat down and talked over matters, so that an agreed boundary line would exist at the River Tamar.

He had started to found the abbey at Mulchelney in Somerset, and intended to found others elsewhere in this beloved England. Milton Abbey in Dorset was also delighted with a relic he had given them, because his fame and popularity were spreading and such relics made places highly popular as pilgrimage centres, which brought in revenue.

When his charters were drawn up he took immense pains to ensure they were witnessed by various sub-kings, so he rode back into Mercia pleased with the way matters were going. If there was one question that still hovered it related to Constantine. It was true the Penrith Treaty still held, giving a peace that area had never known before, but he could not but help wonder whether this would last.

His scribe Rannulf rode with him. He had hesitated to take a new husband away from his bride, but England had to come first and the young man had turned into just about pure gold dust. No day in the saddle was too long for him and Ceorl had trained him beautifully.

Now Aethelstan was heading back into what he thought of as his home territory, where were his treasured friends, Cerdic and Edith, Osburga and Oswald and Egbert. He sensed the younger man's impatience to return to his wife and wondered what it really was like to be so in love. Notwithstanding he was King, he would never know, but he realised his decision made long ago was the correct one. When he thought back to the attempts made on his life, especially from Anlaf, having no heir of his own did not really matter. His half brother Edmund was well into his learning and training, and there would be just a handful of years until he could stand by Aethelstan's side, as king-in-waiting.

He turned to Rannulf riding one length behind and nodded for him to come forward.

'You have your necessary notes?'

'Yes, sire. All in my saddlebags.'

Aethelstan prided himself on being a fast reader, but he was forced to admit he could not match the young scribe's speed for writing. He had been fascinated to learn that certain signs had been memorised for many common words. Rannulf had explained how it was a system invented by Ceorl, but that he had expanded it to suit himself—inexplicable to anyone but the young scribe.

'There'll be many messages to write, then I will be riding to York and will want you with me,' he said warningly. 'It has become too much for your father,' he admitted slowly. 'Even with the medicine woman's salves and supporting bandages. However, when I call my great council I will want all witan members and advisers present from all over my country,' he warned. 'Your father and others may have to ride on ahead.'

Rannulf listened politely and nodded, though he bubbled inside to get home and see his wonderful Osburga. Aethelstan sensed his impatience only just under control, and took pity on him. 'Ride on ahead if you wish,' he said with one of his engaging smiles, 'but don't founder your horse. He's a good one!'

'Can I really, sire?' Rannulf breathed with rising excitement.

'Go on! Clear off and tell the good lady wife I'll be looking forward to a brew of her ale and a sleep in the chamber reserved for me. Go!'

Rannulf went. It was Judith who was first alerted to a rider approaching at a hand gallop by the nearest sentry. She called to her new friend Osburga, and, hearing her voice, Ceorl came out to join them. He was delighted at the friendship that had developed so suddenly between Judith and Osburga, and also more than a little amused at the way Osburga hung on Judith's every word. It had entered his head, in a subtle manner, Judith had begun to treat the much younger girl as a personal acolyte. She spent time talking to her, explaining, showing her plants and methods from which he, as a mere male, was totally excluded. He could only hope and pray her love for Rannulf would rub off to his benefit, because Judith, although friendly and even kind to him, was also aloof at even a remote hint of matrimony.

Rannulf cantered to them, vaulted from his saddle and grabbed his wife, giving her a bear hug. Ceorl watched them and noted Judith did also.

'That could be us,' Ceorl said in a soft voice.

Judith faced him foursquare. 'All right. Yes. But with conditions attached!'

Ceorl blinked with shock then beamed a smile of delight as he hugged her. 'At last! Mine!' he said, then paused with a frown. 'Conditions?' he asked nervously.

'I am what I am,' Judith began. 'A medicine

141

woman. I will always hold myself available to help those who want it. If some day there will be another battle I shall go to the battlefield and . . .' she paused with a secret smile. 'I don't think I'll be going alone, so Rannulf has to do some learning as well.'

Ceorl relaxed. Was that all? He could not envisage a situation now where there would be another great battle. England was one. Treaties had been drawn up and signed, and though there might be some skirmishes now and again—a great battle? Unlikely.

'I agree!' he said quickly and recklessly. 'We want a churchman now to marry us!'

Judith read him and said nothing. He had understood and agreed. How she knew future events she had no idea, and had once mentioned this to the old mother. Her reply had been succinct. 'It is an instinct with some of us. Not exactly for telling the future but some kind of logic from general knowledge and the end results of permutations and political awareness. It is highly developed in you as I have noticed. You were born with it but living with me has developed what is natural to you, which means it will be either a gift or a curse, but you have it and must live with it!'

How true were those wise old words, because Judith knew, no matter what Ceorl might think, or even the king, one day a battle would require help from many like her.

Where, when and the circumstances leading to this she did not yet understand. She just knew it in her bones. Many would die. Blood would flow as never before for a long day, which would never be forgotten.

'You really will marry me?' Ceorl confirmed, bubbling with excitement.

'Do you accept my conditions?' Judith insisted. He was a good man and would never break his word.

'Of course I do!' and Ceorl knew he was on very safe ground now. 'Everyone!' he called as Edith and Cerdic joined the group. 'She has said yes!' and he paused. 'Where is there a priest though?'

Rannulf grinned at him. 'As it happens, there is one riding with the king, who should be here within a few hours,' and he looked at Edith. 'He is looking forward to your best ale and a good night's sleep in the chamber you keep for him!'

'Oh my goodness. I must make sure it's tidy!' And Edith hastily vanished in a rapid swirl of her long skirt while Cerdic spoke for both him and Ceorl.

'What has happened at Exeter and will there be much writing to do?' he wanted to know.

'Quite a bit for both of us, then, after a rest, I think the king plans to ride into South Wales to deal with those other minor kings before heading up to York again. He is definitely going to call a grand council at Colchester.'

'Well, that will be a very first!' Ceorl said thoughtfully, one hand clasped in Judith's. 'Never been done before. I wonder why not.'

'A sound idea though. Clear the air. Sort out problems with general discussions, but with a long ride,' he reflected, 'we oldies might have to leave in advance.'

'I'll help with your knee problems but pick good horses to ride. Short backs, long sloping shoulders and a slow canter are more comfortable than hours trotting and won't exhaust a fit horse!' Judith remarked. 'Also ride with a longer stirrup. Not so much strain on the knees. Let the groin muscles take the strain!' she continued to advise and both men listened to her carefully. She appeared to have the knowledge.

'The king!' a sentry bellowed, and Aethelstan appeared with a churchman, trying to keep up, on a scraggy little horse.

As he dismounted easily Aethelstan beamed at his old friends, delighted to see their faces. Ceorl could not restrain himself and barged forward, dragging Judith with him.

'Sire! Sire!' he cried, his voice throbbing with emotion. 'She's made up her mind! It's a yes!'

Aethelstan stepped forward and slapped him on the back then turned to face Judith, who stood a little uncertain at being the centre of everyone's attention. 'Young lady! Your choice is sound!' Aethelstan said in his very solemn king's voice. And without hesitation he bent forward and kissed one cheek. Judith turned as red as a winterberry and felt ridiculous tears hovering. She gave a deep sniff as he read her emotions.

'This calls for a celebration and feast, and you churchman can do some work and wed this couple. I'll consider myself honoured to be one of the witnesses!' Aethelstan fixed the tired priest with a steady stare then turned his attention to Edith, who scurried forward.

'Your personal chamber is ready, sire, with plenty of hot water for bathing!'

'Splendid. I feel filthy. Afterwards we will be having a wedding. Any chance of a feast, good lady wife, but, first of all, my throat is dry and . . . !' he got no further, because Edith waved and one of the freed females came forward with a brimming tankard, nice and frothy on top.

Aethelstan grabbed it, nearly in rude haste, took a great swallow then drained the rest and finished up smacking his lips with pleasure. 'Now I feel positively civilised. Wash, fresh clothes, clean hair then . . .' he turned to Edith. 'I'm hungry!' he uttered, almost in a plaintive voice.

Everyone had to laugh as Edith escorted him into their very commodious house, while Cerdic hastened to arrange where tents could be struck. He whistled up his housemen to see to the horses and arrange food and drink for a large number of men, also hungry and thirsty.

Rannulf went into Ceorl's house and looked around. It was so very good to be back once more. He opened his bag and dug out copious notes. There was much work and writing to do, and it was possible the king had extra ideas as well. This grand council would take considerable organisation, which obviously would need even more letters. He laid them all out on the table and started to collate them into order. He had grown considerably and there was no resemblance at all to the green youth of early days. He and Osburga shared half of Ceorl's house with him. Would the other part be big enough for him and Judith, or should he start thinking of his own home? It made an interesting question, and it was unlikely events in the near future would give him much time to solve this problem.

Ceorl's mind had functioned on the same lines. 'Thinking of your own place?' he asked as he came in to finger some of the writing skins. What neat penmanship Rannulf had—better than his, really.

'Yes, but only thinking! So much to do!' Rannulf replied.

Ceorl brought him up to date with home events. 'Osburga and Judith have really hit it off. I do believe she's training her in medicine. Won't do any harm, because it's useful to have the skill here.'

146

'Getting married tomorrow or today, Father?'

'This evening, but it will be a quiet affair. Just us few friends. Judith doesn't want a crowd of strangers. Neither do I,' Ceorl explained. Anything to please his darling when he never really thought this day would come. All had been fate since he'd seen her on the battlefield, out of the blue. He smiled quietly to himself. Life was starting to become quite wonderful for someone of his age.

Aethelstan sat at the head of the table and was served a gargantuan meal, which he wolfed down as if starving. Edith's ale was so good, with just the correct bite to its flavour. Even the little priest had mellowed after conducting the marriage service, and he showed he could match his king, drink for drink, with gusto.

The newly wed couple vanished discreetly, and they settled down to a steady drinking session, though they all knew they'd pay in the morning. Aethelstan decided to tarry a few days here. He was so comfortable, felt so much at home with these good people. He knew he must try and fit in a visit to see his half brother Edmund, the king in waiting. It would be only a handful of years before he could stand shoulder to shoulder with him on a battlefield. Sometimes Aethelstan had an uneasy feeling that these days were halcyon ones. He carried a permanent question regarding Constantine's possible plans and activities. Constantine had no love for him, that he knew. At the same time, Aethelstan did understand Constantine's constant worry about being hemmed in by the Norse Irish and losing land to them. Yet that was what the treaty was about. If Constantine wanted help he had only to send a courier to the King of all England, who would respond positively and immediately. Yet he knew he would not. Constantine had resentment because he had been designated as a sub-king. He had been forced to lose face before his own men. Aethelstan gave a shrug and realised he had drunk more than enough ale for the night. With rather unsteady legs he staggered erect and headed for his night chamber. His sleep that night was compounded by ale and satisfaction at how his plans, Constantine excepted, were coming to fruition. What he really looked forward to was his proposed grand council, with everyone possible present, including nobles from the continent. If Constantine jibbed at coming at all, or was morose or distant if he did turn up, it would give an indication for the future. The King of England slept.

Ceorl and Rannulf worked long and hard as scribes, giving Judith and Osburga time alone in which they walked out, escorted by a guard, to view plants. Judith went to great pains with explanations, because she realised she had found a treasure in the younger girl, who had also turned into a great companion, even

148

though still so young.

'One day it will be a battlefield,' Judith told her.

Osburga was puzzled. 'But the country has been unified by the king and is at peace!'

Judith gave a deep sigh. 'Long may it last but . . .' and she let the sentence hang unfinished.

'Do you know something?'

Judith shook her head. 'Not at all. There is just my instinct, which warns me one day I'll be needed and others like me,' and she noted Osburga's puzzled frown. 'Look at it like this. We all have instincts, though ours are not as finely developed as those of the wild animals. Perhaps we had them once, long, long ago, but in this modern life and civilisation it has been bred out of most people.' She paused to collect her thoughts. 'Yet some few people do retain ancient instincts, but are often not aware of this. Take the mother with her baby. Hers are very developed for the safety of the baby.'

'Do you have these?' Osburga asked with fascinated interest.

'Yes, but I did not fully realise this until I started going with the old mother. How it all works I don't know,' she admitted ruefully. 'But I found the longer I lived with her, the more these developed. It may be so with you. Time will tell, but I do say this,' and she turned to look her friend square in the eyes. 'One day there is going to be an enormous, terrible battle. I feel it in my bones, my heart and my head. When it happens I'll leave Ceorl because myself and others will be wanted.'

'And me?' Osburga asked quickly.

Judith patted one shoulder. 'That will be up to you, but you'll see sights the horror of which you'll never forget. You may have a child by then and . . .'

'In which case he or she will be left with my mother. I'll want to be with you. To help. So do what you can to teach me,' she said firmly as a vow. Judith had turned into a wonderful big sister and made her realise how boring her earlier life had been. Now she had Rannulf, a wonderful loving husband, and this fascinating new friend.

Judith was uncertain. Words could be easy to say, even trite, but she knew, despite what the king had managed to do so far, something quite horrendous was on the distant horizon. 'Well, we'll just have to wait and see, won't we?' she ended with a smile and another shoulder pat.

NINE

Aethelstan felt more satisfaction as he rode into his palace at York, with Rannulf nearby. He liked the young man and his brightness. He also marvelled at how a born-and-bred slave had elevated himself through sheer hard work. At the same time, he knew he would forever be in his debt for his life. England owed him much. Between the two of them a relationship had begun to develop. Aethelstan was only a few years the senior, and although separated by royal status an easy friendship was being forged.

They had arrived at York after some fighting in South Wales, encouraging, as Aethelstan put it, more sub-kings to join his alliance. Their next call had been to visit brother Edmund, and that had also been very worthwhile. His half brother was a genuine specimen, well advanced in his martial training, and his tutors spoke highly of his intellectual achievements. When the time came for him to go, Aethelstan was confident Edmund would become a good and popular king. It was just such a shame he had never known wonderful Aunt Aethelflaeda.

'This is Rannulf, my scribe,' he had introduced them, and later on, in private, he had given his brother Rannulf's remarkable background. 'Lean on him a lot. Learn from him too! Because he also saved my life,' which had been another story to relate. Edmund had been enormously impressed and highly interested in this unusual scribe. Aethelstan's sage advice was immediately taken to heart by Edmund, particularly when Aethelstan had added: 'I regard him also as a—friend! Believe me, brother, friends are priceless, though it is not easy for them because of our regal rank.'

They had then ridden to York where his sister still lived. Aethelstan spent private time with her, then walked around the city, flanked by his gesith.

'Trade from here is becoming remarkable. We import and export even from the Byzantine Empire,' Aethelstan had said, then noted Rannulf's frown. 'Geography weak?' he teased.

'Am afraid so, sire!'

'Think of it as the eastern Mediterranean region. At the rate trade is booming here, London will have to look to its laurels!'

Rannulf understood, because since his last visit the city had expanded to become positively crowded. Aethelstan's own coinage was now in circulation and York almost reeked of money and trading affluence, yet he still noted there were some poor people around.

'Yes!' Aethelstan agreed. 'I don't like to find some of my people are poor. I want a charter to be drawn up now, on a legal basis, which states that every man who is poor should receive twenty sheaves of corn from those with decent land of a reasonable size. My royal manors are also to pay an annual charge, which is to go to the poor and needy. There is something else I wish to organise. I wish to donate a good sized plot of my royal land upon which is to be built a hospice, again for the needy. I will not stand by and do nothing when some of my subjects are in distress. Got all that written down?' Aethelstan asked, and peering at his companion marvelled at his shortened form of writing. What a memory he had!

They had paused to permit Rannulf to write on a parchment, used now instead of writing skins, being more practical with a superior finish, resting on his thigh. He gave a grunt of satisfaction, rolled it up, placed it in his shoulder bag and extricated another. It seemed the king was in a dictating frame of mind.

'And another thing, 'Aethelstan continued, 'I have decided that all criminals are to be moved to any part of the country that needs labour until the culprit has paid his dues to our society. Further, I think it's high time all blood feuds were halted. Such an unnecessary waste of life. Let the wergild stand in a blood feud's place. After all, every man does know exactly where he stands for the administration of fines and penalties. I strongly object to thieves of twelve years being executed. I want this age limit to be raised to fifteen years and no arguments about it either. It's my royal command. Every hundred court is to have at least ten men in a tything, to keep law and order, to help to administer my justice. To administer an agreed sentence for offences, twelve good men and true are to be used. I feel cool about the ordeal. It doesn't really prove anything, does it, walking across red-hot coals, leaving feet that then go rotten and kill with the stinking disease? The same as the ordeal of being thrown into water, tied up. So the person drowns even if innocent. Insane, but I suppose it's going to take time to eradicate what I consider to be barbaric and quite pointless exercises that have held sway for generations. My brother agrees with me. He says when he becomes King he will halt all of these, no matter what, so it will help him if I do the groundwork by letting my displeasure be known. Got that lot down too?'

Rannulf scribbled on furiously, then gave a nod. 'Just, sire!' he confirmed.

Aethelstan was delighted. Ceorl had always been good, but there was no doubt Rannulf was far ahead of him now, yet he could not find it in his heart to retire such a long-serving, trusted retainer. Ceorl would have to attend his grand council, which was, he had decided, to be but one of many. Ceorl would simply have to be nursed as the oldie, and Cerdic also, he reminded himself quickly, otherwise they would be insulted. If her beloved man was upset by him, Aethelstan had a shrewd idea that the good lady wife Edith might quickly turn into a spitting wild cat with vicious claws aimed at him. When he had become King it had never entered his head he would have to handle emotional situations with enormous delicacy. He must have a word with Edmund and forewarn him.

'Where was I, scribe?' he grunted. 'I have had wandering thoughts for a short while!'

Rannulf quickly read back his last notes. That was nearly another parchment full. When he did return, he and Ceorl would be working hard again, collating these myriad notes and carefully writing them out in legible longhand. He loved the work though. There was great satisfaction in it, plus the close working with the king. He felt he now knew the king's mind in depth and greatly admired him.

'I'm thirsty!' Aethelstan said suddenly and looked around hopefully.

Rannulf turned to one of the gesith guards and lifted his right arm and made mock drinking movements and nodded at the king. The guard grinned understandingly. He turned and shot into an open doorway of a trader, hissed a request and a young girl vanished for a short while, then returned with a tankard foaming at its top. The guard nodded to the king. The girl dimpled, then handed it over.

'Not having one, scribe?' Aethelstan asked with surprise.

Rannulf shook his head firmly. 'I keep myself on a tight rein because of what happened to my natural father,' he explained.

Aethelstan had not heard this story so Rannulf related what he had learned about how Alcium had ruined his life and even contributed to his own demise.

'I vow that will never happen to me, sire,' Rannulf said strongly.

Aethelstan thought about this for a few brief heartbeats, then nodded. 'Wise object lesson!' he agreed. 'Much as I love a drink of ale I am prudent when and where I take it!'

*　　*　　*

Aethelstan ended up highly delighted. His first grand council had turned into a resounding success, beyond his wildest expectations. There had been so many present the land had mushroomed tents when building accommodation had run short of supply.

All the sub-kings had turned up, even, to his surprise, Constantine. He had gone out of his way to be affable and they had managed to exchange some light remarks. It had crossed Aethelstan's mind to wonder exactly why Constantine had appeared. Was he genuinely interested, in some kind of party mood? Surely this was dubious? Had he come to see for himself just who was on Aethelstan's side for future troublemaking? What exactly was his motive, as it was a long way to ride from his northern position? Did he carry murderous thoughts in his mind? Aethelstan decided to be constantly alert and prudent enough to have members of his personal gesith around when he was with Constantine. He remembered their meeting and knew, without a doubt, Constantine had, for a few heartbeats, considered a wild charge forward to kill him. Yet he had to admit the Treaty of Penrith did still hold. Why did he always have such a large question lodged in his head then?

The continental nobles were all highly delighted with their beautiful wives and came laden with gifts, with which he reciprocated keenly. One valued book was on geometry, a subject that enthralled him but did not appear to interest others, certainly not Rannulf, who, he knew, had shown interest only to be polite. He was pleased with his patronage of the masons, taking an abiding interest in their foundation at York, which would spread in time to all of England, and from now on they would hold an annual meeting in this city. This was important, as the site of the first official lodge back in 926. His agents had all taken the opportunity to visit him with relics and books they had acquired, which further delighted him.

His old friends were also present, as they had left in ample time to ride gently. Cerdic and Ceorl strolled around together leaving Rannulf to do any immediate work.

'So many people!' Cerdic marvelled.

Ceorl nodded, also impressed. To them it was nothing but a fascinating holiday, something they had never had before. They were both now getting crippled with their knee joints, despite Judith's best endeavours.

Both of them realised this would be the one and only council they would be capable of attending, so they listened intently to all the discussions, with subjects usually started by the king. There was nothing acrimonious. All the sub-kings were of mutual agreement, that unification into one country was beneficial to all, because forever, over in Dublin, were the aggressive Norse Irish.

Both were pleased to see Burhred again talking to the king. There was something about the old mercenary that appealed to them, especially when they both thought back to the circumstances of their initial meeting.

'How is my navy?' Aethelstan asked him.

'Ready for whenever you want to use it, sire. I have the men all fit and more than capable. I exercise them regularly and we go to sea in all weathers.'

Aethelstan nodded. This was one tough man, and he knew reliability when he met it. 'I have a feeling in my bones I will need my navy one day,' he commented thoughtfully. 'When and the actual circumstances are hidden from me at present. I just follow my nose!'

'Just send a fast courier, sire, and let me know your exact wishes. I will do the rest,' Burhred told him with a wolfish grin. He too was amazed at how his life had developed since the day a wandering bishop had engaged him and his small party of mercenaries. In many ways, Anlaf had done him a good turn with his treachery.

When the king moved on he strolled over to old friends Cerdic and Ceorl. 'My God,' he thought, 'they have aged suddenly,' but he kept this from his features, instead slapping them on their backs in greeting.

'Been seasick yet?' Cerdic mocked.

Burhred laughed. 'I'm one of the lucky ones,' he told them. 'I'm able to keep control of my stomach in even the stiffest of blows.'

'Some council!' Ceorl said, shaking his head with considerable amazement at so many present, kings in their own right as well as nobles. He was heartily glad to delegate the work to Rannulf, who thrived on it, as he had done at his age. It certainly made their life easier now they had plenty of parchment sheets on which to write. Animal skins, even thin ones, had never been wholly satisfactory. He nearly burst with pride at Rannulf's climb to his current position. He had no objection at all to being relegated to the humdrum copying work at home, because he knew that riding horses no longer had any attraction. He suspected his good pal Cerdic had reached the same conclusion.

These were such good days because even the roaming Danes had diminished in number. Homes and lives were so much safer, though, like all prudent men, he and Cerdic kept well trained guards on duty at all times. The days of savage battles were at an end, and it was

Aethelstan who had sagaciously arranged this in such a skilful way. His domestic life was so sweet. Osburga was ready to produce her first child, but Judith showed no signs of quickening despite his best endeavours. Did Judith, as a medicine woman, know something he did not? This thought kept hovering in his mind, but he knew better than to ask her. She was incredibly secretive regarding her skills. The only person with whom she would discuss these was Osburga, who copied her by keeping her lips shut tight. Even Rannulf had joked about the ladies and their secrets. But then, did it really matter whether Judith had a child or not? He was ageing so rapidly he knew he would never see any child reach adulthood, and it was blindingly obvious Judith lacked deep maternal feelings. Over time this subject slid to the back of his mind and, he knew, would gradually fade into oblivion. It was enough she was his loving wife with ardent companionship. It was true he never forgot the condition she had made for her consent to marry, but this was now irrelevant when England was at peace. Battles had become history only.

They now had some good, gentle years, so when the blow came it was devastating. Cerdic and Ceorl could hardly believe their ears, but Rannulf was unsurprised. He was in constant attendance on the king and had easily followed his line of reasoning. It meant being away from his wife, new baby girl and home for long periods, but Osburga accepted these absences. She was so proud of his position and quietly suspected one day he would be elevated in rank, but she too had a shock. Rannulf was discreet and never related the king's confidences. Right away she consulted with Judith, her adopted big sister, who simply nodded sagely.

'How did you know?' Osburga questioned, deeply puzzled.

Judith could not explain what her instinct had told her was inevitable. She accepted the old mother's comments made so long ago now. It was something with which she had been born, and it was equally obvious it was what Osburga lacked through no fault of her own. A person had it or did not.

Aethelstan walked with Rannulf in privacy, though watched by his gesith. Rannulf made an excellent sounding board. Any comments from him were astute and worth digestion.

'I just knew it was too good to last,' Aethelstan told him.

'Instinct, sire?'

'Plus a shrewd idea of what makes the man tick. Fool he is!' and there was unusual anger in Aethelstan's voice. 'So be it!'

'War, sire?'

'Very much so, and this time all out. Sea as well as land. Torn up the treaty. I'll teach him!' Aethelstan rumbled. 'My army will go

161

up there and really crush him this time, as well as my navy. Come what may afterwards. I will not have my unified England split apart again because of Constantine!'

Rannulf tactfully stayed silent. He had never seen the king so furious before, then it hit him. Judith and Osburga! He knew in his bones his wife would follow her adopted sister, just as he was fully aware Judith would not be kept away. Did Ceorl understand? He kept this new worry to himself, then realised the two would most likely be the safest pair on a battlefield. Even a madman would not lift a finger against a healing woman, but he did not like it one bit. What made it worse was the knowledge he would not be able to object. Osburga had a strong will and she had become so close to Judith. Perhaps even too close, but he could not bear to row with his beloved.

Aethelstan chewed his lip thoughtfully. 'I'll have writing for you, as I want my Welsh king allied with me. At the same time I'll want close liaison with Burhred, because I intend to strike on land and sea at the same time. It means working out how long to get the army up north, so that Burhred has time to get in position for a joint strike. I'll come back with you now, to my second home, so I can discuss all with Cerdic and Ceorl.'

Rannulf knew he did not mean one of his palaces, but the private chamber reserved for him alone by Edith, for whom he had such admiration.

Aethelstan was not entirely finished though. He enjoyed confiding in his young scribe and realised it was time he elevated him in rank to Earldorman. With only a few more years he could take his place on his personal witan.

Rannulf had also been thinking on his feet. 'What about some hostage-taking, sire?' he asked quietly.

Aethelstan blinked and beamed with pleasure. 'My thoughts exactly, scribe!' and he grinned. 'That would certainly concentrate minds, wouldn't it? And it's quite legitimate in wartime too. Even Mother Church would not object!'

'Back home then, sire?'

'Yes, on our way today. I want to toss it all to Cerdic and your excellent father. Let's inform my gesith where I wish to go—like yesterday!'

They rode hard and fast, stopping only to change horses, and within seemingly no time they thundered into Aethelstan's favourite second home. Both king and scribe were young, fit and strong, but even they were glad to empty saddles, as was the gesith.

His friends all came to greet their king. Edith took one look at sweaty faces, vanished inside and had a servant return with their home-brewed ale for all. Tankards were swiftly replenished by men who were now more tired than they cared to admit.

'Baths!' Edith told her female servants. 'For all, too. I'll not feed sweaty, smelly males at my table. All of you go and clean up. That includes you too!' she rasped to Aethelstan's gesith. 'Move! Go follow the women servants. Now!' she barked like a senior soldier. She was hastily and thankfully obeyed.

So it was much later, well into the evening, before Aethelstan sat with his old witan, which included Rannulf.

'Before I start I have one solemn duty to perform, with all you as witnesses. Ceorl, you will write the charter of this first thing in the morning, with the appropriate land deed.' He looked around. Cerdic, Ceorl, Oswald and Egbert wondered what was coming now, because their king was full of surprises.

'From this moment onwards my scribe Rannulf is elevated to the rank of earldorman. He is to be given, in writing, an appropriate land holding, which deed Ceorl will draft right away!'

Rannulf was stunned into shocked silence while his companions slapped his back enthusiastically in congratulation.

'I don't know what to say, sire,' Rannulf murmured in a low voice, enormously touched and acutely embarrassed. He pulled a face at his king and Aethelstan understood his emotion. It was a huge distance from slave to noble. An out-of-the-question distance, and when Rannulf had set out on his personal journey of life, one impossible even to consider. Yet it had happened! To him! Slave born and bred! He simply sat in dumbfounded silence.

Aethelstan took pity on him and related his news. 'I knew that treaty holding was too good to be true. Now I want definite action by land and sea at the same time, so careful calculations are required. Also I want a small, secretive snatch squad to grab one of Constantine's sons, to be held as hostage in my court. He'll be well looked after and educated, but my hostage. It needs reliable, quick-thinking, bold men. Not young hotheads. About three of them. Any ideas, friends?'

'Yes, sire. Those two wandering churls who dealt with the earlier problem,' and Cerdic flashed a look at Aethelstan, who nodded thoughtfully. 'The father and son, Aidan and Edred. You have their oaths and they are well versed in roaming and spying out situations and,' Cerdic frowned, 'also Hoel. No man will ever be more loyal and willing than he, after the bishop murder!'

'Arrange it, but total secrecy!' Aethelstan warned.

TEN

It was decided Cerdic would speak to Hoel, Edred and Aidan, while Ceorl would draft out an earldorman's deed of land. His other men would involve themselves with the sheer logistics of moving an army and navy to attack on a set day. Much would depend upon the weather as well as the problem of moving enough food for hungry warriors.

Aethelstan spoke again. 'As to those Welsh sub-kings, they pay tribute to me and I set this rather high on purpose. Now send messages to them that I expect them to join my army and will then decrease my tribute demands,' he grinned. 'Everyone likes to save money when possible, so there should be no problem there. At the same time I want couriers to go to my new brothers-in-law on the continent for their warriors. This must be a strong victory once and for all. Everyone with me?'

Rannulf wrote fast but Cerdic frowned. Ceorl sat, not exactly in a daze, but he did nothing, contributed not one word and sat with eyes downcast. 'Now what's the matter with him?" Cerdic asked himself. He must speak to him when he could and his chance came when Aethelstan stood, obviously satisfied with his orders, and left his men to get on with it.

Cerdic nodded to Ceorl and strolled aside.

'What's eating you?' he asked bluntly.

Ceorl's face was a picture of misery. 'Judith!'

Cerdic failed to understand. 'She ill?' was his first thought.

'I wish it were something as simple as that!' Ceorl replied heavily. 'No! It's the coming battle. She'll leave me to go up there. I know it. I just know it, and there's little I can do to stop her because of the agreement I made when she said she'd marry me.'

'Oh!' was all Cerdic could manage, but his mind raced. Did that mean Osburga would go too? The two had become almost too close for his liking at times, but Edith had laughed at him when he mentioned this. 'Just a normal girl's friendship for confidences. After all, you men develop close male drinking pals. Stop fussing, do!'

He had no answer but now could feel for his old pal Ceorl. The trouble was, Edith would dote on looking after her first grandchild, and he supposed no one could be safer on a battlefield than medicine women, but he did not care for his daughter being involved.

'I have no solution to that one, friend. You'll just have to grin and bear it or alienate Judith for all times,' he replied slowly. 'It might even end up in divorce,' he warned carefully. 'Surely better what you have, on her terms, than lose and have nothing at all.'

'Talk is cheap at times,' Ceorl rumbled,

167

but knew Cerdic was right. His hands were well and tightly tied. All he could do was bear it with grace and live in hope. He was so old now, more so than Cerdic, and a long ride up north might even kill him from exhaustion. With a thoroughly miserable mind he had to force himself to attend to the king's work.

At the same time, Judith was stuck with her own quandary. The coming battle was what she had known as inevitable, and her problem was Osburga. She had no doubts the younger girl was genuine and would not hesitate to come with her, but, at the same time, she had come to realise Osburga lacked what she could only describe as 'it'. There was no natural instinct in her. It was during many periods of reflection that Judith had to take herself sternly to task. She lived in a superb home, with every conceivable comfort and a husband who adored her, but herself? She was honest enough to admit she felt no flaring love for him, because, after all, what exactly was love? When she watched Cerdic with his joy she knew her marriage lacked this, on her side, and through no fault of Ceorl's. Perhaps there was something amiss or unnatural with her?

She found herself, on many occasions now, reflecting on those wandering days with the old mother. In the wet, cold winter months they had not been comfortable periods, so why did she find herself yearning for them with such wistfulness? She could not understand herself when she now had every modern comfort a person could wish for, except the ability to roam at will, as and when her spirit craved this. Was it the freedom of those days when they answered to no one? Was it more natural to her temperament? Were those days the reason she had been born and bred? She could remember nothing about her parentage, except the old mother had once said she came from a distinguished line of medicine women. How did the old mother know that? She knew the old mother was dead. Some day a person might stumble across a hidden hut and inside would be her skeleton, but she had lived, wild and free for sixty-five summers.

That night Ceorl sat on the edge of their bed and spoke heavily. 'I adore you,' he began, 'more than you me. You've no idea of the wonder and glory when I discovered you on that battlefield, after searching for so long. I realise I'm so much older than you, but I worship you, Judith. If you ever left me for good . . .' and he halted again while two tears trickled down his cheeks. 'I know you'll be off to the battlefield. I beg—please come back to me. What you do after I've gone will be up to you, but while I live, be mine!'

Judith's blue eyes held his face steadily. 'I'll come back. That I vow!' and now *her* voice became husky. Deep down, did she deserve this adoration? This was such a good man. There was no way she could hurt him, yet—

her instinct prodded. Ceorl was as naturally good as King Aethelstan. The king was so intelligent, educated and cultured, they were two of a kind, and sometimes when she thought of the king and Ceorl she felt sadness. As yet, she was still unclear what this predicted for either man, but it was a pain in her heart, still a bit nebulous, but present nevertheless. Only time would explain to her instincts.

The next day Osburga grabbed her when she appeared. 'I'm coming with you,' was her simple announcement. 'I've told Rannulf. He doesn't like it but he'll have to put up with it. After all, he'll be there as the scribe! Edith will look after our child.'

Judith took her time in replying. 'Very well,' she agreed, 'but it won't be at all nice. You simply have no idea of the horrors of battlefield wounds, and your feelings will count for nothing. You will not be sick. You will not swoon. You will not cry out. You will keep your features impassive and under control at all times, or answer to me in person,' she warned, and her voice had a hard edge. 'You will be there to give aid and succour to many who are going to be in agony. Grown men, even, crying for their mothers. You will not help a man to the spirit world without consulting me first. If you make one wrong move, I'll have you removed forcibly. Do you understand?'

Osburga was taken aback. This was another

Judith. Hard and uncompromising, almost dangerous. She swallowed, then nodded firmly. This was what she wanted to do. She could not give battle herself, she was untrained with weaponry, unlike the great Lady of Mercia who lived before her time. 'I understand. I will obey. I only want to help—and be near to Rannulf,' she admitted slowly.

Judith permitted herself a slow smile of approval. At least she had been truly honest. 'We will ride this time and leave before the army. We will live off the land, so bring some hunting equipment as well as your bag of herbal remedies. Always in the past, the old mother and I walked. It will be a change to ride, but we pick good horses. We will depart quietly and suddenly. No one will know. All of us who attend such affairs work like this. Secrecy is our badge of office!'

*   *   *

Aethelstan had known it would take time to move his army northwards to coincide with his navy's position. Time in which Constantine could pick a battlefield to suit himself. There had been many calculations with a fleet of well-mounted couriers, ready to ride at short notice with royal instructions.

Ceorl had stayed at home, unhappy but realistic. Cerdic had made the journey with Oswald and Egbert. Rannulf was in his usual

171

position, just one horse length behind his king, backpack filled with parchments and writing powder to be made into ink.

'So!' Aethelstan drawled, eyeing the vast army camped ready to attack him. He swiftly calculated the opposition, considered the forces at his disposal and worked out his plan of action. The three older men with Rannulf stayed well in the background as non-combatants, but they were all prudently armed with stabbing spears and good shields. He calculated the fight would be the next day, which suited him perfectly. 'Put out good scouts for tonight. Make sure the men are fed and watered. Now what about the snatch squad?'

Rannulf and Cerdic waited alongside him, and Cerdic spoke for both of them. 'They moved off taking their own directions, sire. Hoel, Aidan and Edred. I ordered them to cherish the boy, and if he's frightened, which he will be, to turn it into a game. To take him to Tamworth for the time being and let good women fuss over him. I've also said he's to have the best tutors and not those who believe in using the stick, the best food and dress, as if he's your personal son. In short he is to be cherished.'

'Good!' Aethelstan grunted, then noted an unhappy look on his scribe's face. 'Now what?' he wondered. 'Problems, scribe?'

'Yes, sire, and there's nothing I can do

without a thundering row!' and Rannulf pointed to one side.

Aethelstan spun around, stared and understood. At a distance but visible to his sharp eyes he saw two female forms. Medicine women! He swung his horse around and trotted over with Cerdic and Rannulf at his heels. He halted one horse length away and Judith and Osburga both eyed him silently.

'So, ladies. You have come to follow your calling,' he said heavily. 'I'm afraid your skills will be needed!' and he turned to Cerdic. 'Pick two good men, older ones, and when we've won our battle they are to escort the healers and do their bidding,' he ordered calmly. Some injuries would be so horrific it was kinder to run a sword through a man's heart, to give him instant relief from incredible agony.

Judith's eyes held his and she nodded with approval. Osburga did not yet understand. Rannulf and Cerdic did, and they also approved the king's foresight, but he was experienced in battle. So worthy to be the King of England.

'Do you have rations?'

Again it was Judith who answered as the leader. 'Yes, sire! We have also set snares and have caught two conies. One we will roast for tonight with herbs sprinkled freely,' and her eyes twinkled. As if she'd come without food!

Aethelstan read her unspoken thought and grinned. He should have known better than to

173

ask, he reminded himself. After another brief nod, he turned and rode back with his faithful friends. Later, when fires blazed and men ate, he gathered his friends around with all of his gesith.

'Tomorrow is to be different,' he started carefully. 'No men held in reserve.'

He saw shock on all of their faces, so Aethelstan hastened to explain different tactics. 'I am going to be the sea,' he began carefully. Again he met blank faces and frowns with deep bewilderment.

'The sea comes in remorselessly. Nothing and no man can stop its progress. We do the same. An all-out frontal assault, which does not stop for anything until the enemy cries for our mercy. We fight on foot and in a steady, advancing line of weaponry. No running forward for men to be cut down individually. No shouting and the issuing of personal challenges. That all takes energy, which should be used for the actual battle. Also, a steadily advancing line that stops for nothing will, I calculate, put the fear of God into that lot,' and he nodded in the direction of where the enemy waited. 'He's picked the battlefield but it will do us too. It's flat. I have not been able to see anything like stones or hidden gullies to bring men down. Also, by advancing in such a remorseless, steady line every man can watch out for his neighbour. This is important to men who lead detachments, so they are to be briefed thoroughly. It is vital every man knows my plan. Any questions?' and Aethelstan looked around expectantly.

There was total silence while they digested his orders, then heads began to nod with approval. It would certainly be different, which appealed.

'If we did our sums right the navy will strike tomorrow, up as far as Caithness if they want. They can do all the mayhem they like and loot to their satisfaction, but any relics and books come to me for the Church and monasteries.'

'We calculated carefully, sire,' Cerdic told him thoughtfully. 'We allowed leeway for any bad weather at sea. I've worked it out that your navy has been in position for a few days now, just waiting for tomorrow to make their move.'

Heads nodded in unison and Aethelstan was satisfied. 'Now we will eat. Check the sentries are rotated, though I doubt the enemy will try a sneak night attack, but it's prudent to take precautions.' And he stood. Well satisfied with all, he would retire shortly to his tent and check his chain mail, helmet, and his aunt's sword, then up with the dawn and break his night's fast with a light meal.

He did exactly that. Satisfied he felt clean, he donned his long-sleeved silk shirt, over this went his long-sleeved very thin leather tunic, then chain mail down to his knees. He protected his legs with pads and hefted his helmet and shield. Outside, dawn had broken, and he cast a look at the sky. His direction was east to the enemy, and he grinned. It should be a sunny day, which meant the sun's rays would land on his silver coloured chain mail and dazzle approaching warriors. So far, it was all going very well. Certainly sun on his mail would be an added bonus.

Aethelstan surveyed the long line of warriors who were now keyed up, almost agitated, to start fighting. They had discipline, though Aethelstan knew they could not hope to match that of the old Roman legions, but they did wait, looking at him with tenseness, just poised for the first move from him to start. Their bloodlust was at fever pitch. That many would not see another dawn never entered their heads. Death was something that happened to the other man. Not them.

He looked ahead where a ragged line advanced in spurts, shouting and waving their weapons, bawling what they intended to do. 'Good!' Aethelstan told himself. 'Start to burn up your energy before you've struck one blow!'

He waited a little while longer, then stepped forward purposefully, sword drawn, shield firm in his left hand and arm. His line eagerly moved with him but he was pleased to see they kept good station. Then they met. Weapons slashed into action. Shields clashed. Voices roared and blood flowed.

Aethelstan used his sword perfectly,

sometimes with a cut and slash, while other blows plunged. His gesith moved with him on both flanks, wounding and killing. Men fell on both sides, but Aethelstan concentrated on those who faced him. He dare not throw a sideways look because the next enemy flung himself forward, eager to take out the king. Two blows did get through to clash against his mail, but these perpetrators died instantly. Twice he was jolted and had to readjust his balance, but his right arm and killing sword continued flashing action followed by gouts of blood. He used his shield dexterously, as with eyes narrowed and calculating he made a slow remorseless advance, his men with him. It was all violent action and noise, screams of rage and pain.

A lot of energy was now being used as the pace increased, blows became swifter and more men fell. Aethelstan stepped back half a pace and flashed a quick look to right and left. He saw that his gesith line now had gaps in it, and he gritted his teeth to plunge forward once more, his powerful sword slashing with very rapid strokes, enough to make men retreat before him. This rallied his remaining gesith, who advanced with him when quite suddenly he realised the enemy was backing en masse. 'Charge!' he roared and now they all broke into a faster pace. A killing wave of powerful men demonstrated they were quite unstoppable. The enemy began to retreat faster, turning and stumbling in their haste to find safety, many of them chopped down by this manoeuvre.

Aethelstan looked ahead and then to his right. Immediately he spotted Constantine with just a handful of men around him. He plunged forward striking a path for himself with his sword, then faced his enemy, his sword now horizontal and ready to kill.

'Die or cede!' he challenged.

Constantine knew he had no choice again. Two couriers had reached him with devastating news. A cherished younger son had been snatched and taken unawares as hostage. Every bit as bad was the news that Aethelstan's navy had attacked and were looting wildly. They had even gone as high as Caithness, which meant the king there would blame him, Constantine, for what was happening. He glared his barely contained fury and knew he had no choice. He lifted his sword then plunged it into the soil and stood bare handed to face whatever was now to come. Olaf had been correct. This was no handsome youth. This was indeed a devil king whose face now wore an implacable mask, which did not bode well for him.

Aethelstan though understood magnanimity. Moving slowly, driving home the point, he casually sheathed his sword and likewise stood bare handed. Two kings faced each other while around them the ground was stained with blood, hacked off limbs and men crying for help, as women began to appear and move around them. He opened his hands palms upwards in the universal gesture of peace and reconciliation, though he knew he would never trust this man again.

'Shall we move and let the women do what they can?' he asked quietly, and with a deep sigh Constantine agreed.

Osburga was appalled. She had thought she knew what to expect, but never this. She flashed a look at Judith who pointed to one man with a hideous arm gash.

'Clean it up. Put herbs on it. Sew it up but make sure you insert a drainage tube!' Judith ordered. Over the last few weeks they had collected many stems from thick grasses, which were then cut to appropriate lengths, because the tubes were hollow. They made perfect drainage tubes for the flesh wounds, with a reasonable chance of some recovery, provided the germs had not been able to enter, which caused the rotting, stinking disease.

Judith herself walked among the wounded, conscious of two swordsmen at her rear, and now and again she would turn to them with a tiny nod. Some men were beyond anybody's help. It was kinder to dispatch them from their misery. There were very few capable of being helped, because the wounds from swords and battleaxes were quite horrendous. Helmets split, skulls opened until the brains

179

showed. Limbs were hacked off, legs as well as arms, and there were even some unfortunate warriors whose upper bodies had been hit by a lethal, powerful battleaxe. She had seen it all before. Now and again she cast a look at Osburga, and was pleased to see that at least she was controlling her emotions.

Aethelstan walked over to her with the defeated king, because on a battlefield every man was treated the same, no matter on which side he had fought.

'Bad?' Aethelstan asked quietly.

Judith nodded. 'I think it is as bad as I have ever seen,' she replied, and her eyes went from one king to the other, blaming them equally. Both men flinched under her penetrating and accusing glower. 'Satisfied, the pair of you?' she asked caustically, then turned her back on them and walked away to help someone else, if she could.

Aethelstan faced Constantine. 'She's right, you know!' he said rather coldly, because all this was of Constantine's doing. Constantine had nothing to say, partly because he accepted the truth of her words and also because he was fuming internally at this second defeat, plus the hostage-taking of a son. He wished he had it in him to draw a knife and plunge it into Aethelstan's body, but it would only rebound against the chain mail and he was very aware they were being followed by half a dozen of Aethelstan's personal gesith. He swallowed heavily to control himself, acutely aware he was not a young man anymore. He was now starting to head towards sixty years, whereas this young man could give him many. It was all so grossly unfair and he had not the faintest idea what he could do to remedy this situation in general. He fought a valiant internal battle with himself and managed to fix a bland expression on his features.

'My son?'

Aethelstan switched a pleasant look on his face and patted one shoulder reassuringly. 'Your son will be looked after and cherished as if my son. He will be treated as royal, educated and dressed, as well as tutored in all weapons, and when you do next see him you will probably be delighted.'

'When will that be?'

'Who knows?' Aethelstan replied bluntly. 'In the interim I will be pleased if you will attend some of my courts as my very welcome guest.'

Constantine was forced to admit to himself later he had never before heard an order given with such delicacy, and with a small sigh he nodded.

'I intend to go down to Buckingham to do some business, and I will be pleased if you will witness my charters with the Welsh kings, who will also be present,' Aethelstan informed him coolly.

'Will my son be there?' Constantine wanted

to know.

'Who knows?' Aethelstan riposted. 'Perhaps it is going to depend upon how well he does with his lessons, whether his tutors will agree to his absence.'

They both turned automatically to watch the various medicine women, eight of them now. They wandered from warrior to warrior, and both of them noted very few received medical treatment. The majority of them were dispatched with the sword.

'War is a bad business for the run-of-the-mill warrior,' Aethelstan commented thoughtfully, and for once Constantine had to agree. They looked at each other. They would never be friends, that was quite out of the question, but they could both feel for the rank-and-file warrior who was, when all was said and done, only obeying their orders. 'Will you feed with me tonight?'

Constantine nodded. He was forced to admit again this younger king's manners were quite exemplary. At another time, perhaps in another age, they might be able to develop a rapport and even genuine friendship.

ELEVEN

It seemed a long time to Osburga before they could turn and ride for home, escorted by Cerdic, Rannulf and some others from their region. She was quiet, even Rannulf had difficulty getting words from his wife, and he looked anxiously at Judith. Shortly, after crossing a river, he grabbed the opportunity to ride with her. 'I'm having a job to get speech from Osburga,' he explained with genuine worry.

Judith smiled sympathetically. 'First of all she has had what I suppose is called a culture shock, and secondly the actual sight of a battlefield is enough to upset anyone with a heart. I remember how dreadful it was for me the first time. No amount of warnings or conversation can prepare for the real thing. The trouble is, with our modern warfare, the injuries received are so horrific. So many limbs just chopped off, to be dodged when walking. It's not just the blood that's around but the body parts scattered everywhere.'

Rannulf digested this, and riding one horse length behind, Cerdic was also well tuned in. Judith decided to give it to him straight, for his own peace of mind and his future.

'With the best will in the world, Osburga lacks that important little something. I would

183

never take her on as my acolyte, like the old mother did with me. What she does know and can do is ideal for the home and surroundings. Battlefields? Never!'

'You'd not take her again?' Rannulf asked with rising hope.

'Definitely not. If I need a learner to train I'll go elsewhere, but I will not take your wife. You should get her pregnant again!' she told him bluntly.

This was music to Rannulf's ears and also those of Cerdic. What his joy would say he had no idea, except he knew he would back the scribe. He had a strong suspicion Ceorl would also concur. There might be some arguments but Judith had spoken and on this subject she became their queen.

Osburga relapsed into an even deeper silence at overhearing, and she looked ruefully at Judith. 'I heard,' she said.

Judith nodded. 'Just remember what I have taught you for home cures. Always know where to find maggots to put on wounds. Under old logs, rotting bodies—animals or men—anywhere that stinks of putrefaction They are the very best thing for eating rotting flesh, though even the bravest warrior is inclined to pull a face when he realises creepy crawlies are eating him!' she warned firmly. 'Just carry on with the treatment. For home medicine treatments you are fine!' she praised.

Osburga was scrupulously honest at all

times and understood the significance of Judith's words. Part of her was hurt but the major section of her heart felt relief. She threw her friend a nod then turned to ride with Rannulf.

'Hello you!' she said brightly, and it was not forced. 'Nice to have my husband away from his parchments again. I won't be going with Judith anymore,' she told him gently. 'I'm not good enough.'

'Do you mind? Are you hurt?'

Judith shook her head firmly. 'Not in the least. I'm going to be a home girl. Fancy making another baby?' she asked and dimpled over at him.

Rannulf laughed with relief and pleasure. 'I'm all for it!'

Cerdic felt no shame at his eavesdropping. This was something good and positive. 'Let's ride for home!' he shouted. 'No more of this genteel clip-clopping along!' and he rammed his heels into his horse's flanks, who sprang into a canter of annoyance but then settled down to a gait that would gobble up the miles. He knew he would be incredibly stiff in the morning, with rigid knees, but the morning was another day.

They changed horses a number of times and rested overnight then carried on. 'Where is the king?' Rannulf wanted to know. The last he had seen of him was talking to Constantine. Before he could ask what the king needed Cerdic had chased him away with a blunt 'Home!' which had delighted him, and Osburga had accompanied them.

'He's going to Tamworth to check on his hostage, then I suspect he'll wander down to us before he starts travelling his realm again. I know he likes Tamworth because it was his aunt's favourite base, but he also has affection for Malmesbury. Told me once that is where he wishes to be buried,' Cerdic explained, then groaned. 'I'm heartily sick of saddles and horses. I wonder if one day our descendants will be able to travel without going within a mile of a saddle. I swear I'm getting bow legged!' he grumbled with a passion. 'You can grin now but one day you'll be old and suffer the same if you keep on breathing long enough!'

Rannulf laughed aloud and with mischief pushed his own mount into a faster pace. Cerdic swore lustily at his back then resigned himself to copy. 'Bloody kids!'

They clattered into their home territory, and Edith, Ceorl and the workers were ready to greet them, forewarned by an outlying sentry.

'My joy. Get rid of this beast and anything like him with four legs! And lead me to a proper chair with your ale. I feel shattered!' he groaned, and Edith hugged him with sympathy. He really was far too old to be gallivanting around like this, and she vowed to have a quiet word with the king again when the next opportunity arose. If Ceorl could stay and work at home then so could her beloved Cerdic.

Ceorl's face lit up in a magnificent smile as he strode forward, grabbed Judith in a bear hug and kissed her with devotion. 'You *did* come back!'

'I said I would. Remember?' Judith said gently.

'I was afraid that . . .' and Ceorl's words died away as two tears flowed down his cheeks again. He told himself he had become a sentimental idiot, and to control himself, as she tucked her arm in his, he walked into their part of his home while Rannulf escorted Osburga. He was filled with gratitude at how matters had come to a positive and satisfactory conclusion. Now to get down to the important business of making another baby. Osburga would not be leaving with Judith ever again, so perhaps the battle had been good for him—as well as the king.

*   *   *

Aethelstan was not quite so certain. He knew Constantine reverberated with resentment, which could soon turn into dangerous hatred. This was the second time the King of England had bested him in battle, and he knew his stock would have plummeted with his warriors.

187

Indeed, it was highly likely many of them would be thinking of leaving to give their oaths to a more victorious king, which, of course, was within their rights as long as they handed back to him the horses and equipment he had given them after accepting their oaths. He was straight enough to admit he would, if in their boots, transfer his allegiance to a more promising king, but it stuck in his throat enough to gag him. A king without warriors became a non-king, just a queer almost macabre joke. But what exactly could he do right now? A precious younger son was this man's hostage and his older son, although coming on well in his martial training, was not yet ready for action. There was his age too. He was heading to the wrong side of his fifties, while this devil king bristled with youth. It was all so grossly unfair, but he switched an amenable smile on his face, though it failed to reach his eyes, which Aethelstan's sharp, more youthful ones, did not miss. 'Duplicity is it?' Aethelstan asked himself, and was even amused. This man was next door to becoming desperate. 'I'll enjoy your company with me as my important guest at my courts,' he said aloud. 'Perhaps you will honour me by signing some of my charters as I make new laws?'

Constantine snapped a curb on his temper. 'If this is your wish?'

'It certainly is, and as a token of my esteem for you will you accept my bracelet to wear?'

and he pulled one off his left arm and handed it over. Constantine was quite taken aback. This was not a gesture he would have thought of making, and he was enormously impressed with such a valuable bracelet made cleverly from gold and silver. It did cross his mind to wonder if he might be misjudging this young king. After all, he was the loser, and most victorious kings would have handed over a swipe with the cutting edge of their sword, not given a magnificent present.

'Why thank you!' Constantine replied, and slid the bracelet on one arm, stared at it and admired the skill which had made it. 'I've not seen one so beautifully crafted before!'

'My pleasure, brother king!' and Aethelstan was pleased. He did not have a mean hair on his body, and if this valuable bracelet helped towards peace it was to the good. 'But,' he told himself, 'I'm going to slip someone in among his men to spy!' He would copy Anlaf to keep up to date with information. He must speak to Cerdic in private when he could.

Until then he would ride to Tamworth and see his hostage, then go again down into Mercia before heading for Malmesbury. Once more his gesith would be riding long and hard with him, yet he looked forward to seeing his personal friends, and he wished to talk confidentially with Cerdic. Such a wise, older man with shrewd ideas, to which he always listened carefully. He had often found his thoughts ran parallel with his own, which was encouraging.

It was a few days later, staying in his personal chamber, fussed over by Edith and thoroughly enjoying the experience, that he nodded to Cerdic as he went for a stroll. Cerdic immediately understood and walked with him.

'I don't trust Constantine at all,' Aethelstan began. 'I've beaten him twice, which simply must fester and rankle. Not that he'll do anything underhand while I have his son. It's after, when I return him, that bothers me.'

Cerdic gave a snort. 'Don't return him then. Keep him, sire!'

'I can't do that forever. Unfair to his mother,' Aethelstan replied with a grimace. 'Never let it be said I waged war on females.'

'Don't agree, sire!' Cerdic replied bluntly. 'Don't they say that all is fair in love—and war?'

'You're a tough old bloodthirsty rogue, I think!' Aethelstan said with a smile.

'A man fights to win with any weapon, especially against a man who has twice tried it on and will do so again, if he gets but half a chance!'

Aethelstan pulled a face. 'Your advice has always been so sound, but I know I could not break a mother's heart!'

Cerdic did not like this, but he had given his advice. He could do no more. In one way he could understand Aethelstan's feelings, but he was practical. He too did not trust Constantine one iota, but his king had spoken.

'Do you have special ideas, sire?'

Aethelstan nodded. 'And this is where I want your help. I wish to do an Anlaf, but it might be for a long period of time.'

Cerdic understood in a flash, and this was an action with which he agreed wholeheartedly. 'Slip in spies, sire?'

'Yes, but it will have to be done very carefully for the men's own safety,' Aethelstan started. 'It's no good men going up there to give their oaths to Constantine. That wouldn't work right now. They have given their oaths to me. If they chop and change we could end up with the Rannulf situation being duplicated. Also, after this second defeat by me, it wouldn't surprise me if some of Constantine's men don't wander down to give their oaths to me, especially if they are of the looting fraternity,' he said dryly.

'That's very true, sire. We must think this through very carefully. The scheme must be quite perfect, needing men who can live up there, without giving their oaths to Constantine, but also able to communicate with us at all times, when they have information,' Cerdic murmured. They strode on, going nowhere in particular, just moving to help their thought processes.

'Those men who gave their oaths to you

191

after Edwine's drowning,' Cerdic said: 'the only reason they did this was that the weather was entering the cold months and they thought more of their creature comforts.'

'What are they like as fighters?' Aethelstan wanted to know.

'Good men with the spear and javelin,' Cerdic confirmed. Only royals and nobles carried and used swords. 'But on the other hand, nothing outstanding. Not top class enough for your gesith, sire.'

Aethelstan frowned in deep thought. 'They must have a good cover, an excuse for being present in the north,' he murmured.

Cerdic gave a tiny half nod. 'Hunters!' he said suddenly. 'And skin tanners!' he suggested.

'That's a good thought, but can they hunt well?'

'Yes, sire. They *are* good hunters. Obviously had practice during the times when they had to live off the land, when there was nowhere for them on the estates. They were the men who killed those stags you gave to Constantine's men after the first battle!'

'Is that so!' Aethelstan halted and faced him. 'Where are they now?'

'Probably still up north, looting.'

'Get them back—like yesterday!'

'Two can play at that game, sire,' Cerdic pointed out.

'True, but unlikely while I have his son!'

Aethelstan rejoined. 'However, we'll be prudent. If men arrive wanting me to take their oaths check them out thoroughly. But I want to speak to those churls personally.'

Cerdic nodded and ran his mind over the available couriers and the time lag. Probably take a week to get them back, because first they had to be found. He hastened off to see to this new task, his mind spinning with all the permutations. He would have a chat with Ceorl first, who had a good head on him.

Aethelstan stayed one night and thoroughly enjoyed Edith's fussing, then rode off with his gesith to Malmesbury. He would call in again on his way back, while he made detailed plans to go to Buckingham, where Constantine would attend to witness his signature. Fogan of Strathclyde and Hywel Oder would also attend as his guests, and they too could witness his charters. After that he knew he must go to Cirencester for more business. There was so much he was anxious to do for his country and people now he had achieved unification, but it all took time. It would not be all that long before the miserable cold months set in, which, with heavy snow, would make travelling very difficult.

Ceorl was thoughtful after Cerdic explained their king's plans. As it stood, it seemed reasonable, and certainly the two men could not give fresh oaths to Constantine. He would be highly suspicious to start with, because his own men must have begun to desert him. They certainly could not afford another situation like Rannulf had experienced all that time ago. Hunters? Yes, possible, he thought, but were they at all literate to get messages down in writing with a courier? Should there not be some other type of code? The more he thought about this the more he considered it viable. What type of code? Right now, he had no idea at all. Then it hit him and he turned to Cerdic.

'A code. Something plain, simple, innocuous, quite utilitarian!' he stated with his eyes hard and glinting.

Cerdic frowned, bewildered. 'What on earth are you on about?' he grated.

'Like an ordinary belt. No one would wish to steal that but its very appearance could sound the alarm!' Ceorl explained a little testily.

Cerdic turned this over in his mind then nodded slowly. 'Brilliant!' he praised. 'We all wear belts either over or under our tunics. Just a plain run-of-the-mill belt but with some distinguishing mark known only to us. A particular buckle?'

Ceorl shook his head. 'Better to have something like a dagger slash on it. All belts get rough treatment, just because they are belts. Get Rannulf to put one of his secret short words on it that just he, me, you and the king recognise!'

'Perfect! As soon as the king returns we'll

tell him!'

Aethelstan soon returned. He felt religiously refreshed and also, he admitted to himself, he missed his old friends very much, especially Cerdic and Ceorl. They had been with him so long now, through all his trials and tribulations. It was true he had witans to advise all over his country, especially at London and York, but they were just that. His witan advisers, not personal friends with whom he could let his hair down, speak his mind and laugh. They had become the big brothers he'd never had, and if he could have made them royal he would have done so. Rannulf too was valuable. Not just because of his skill as the senior scribe but because his links also were old and valued. After all, it was through Rannulf he still lived. There was a rapport between both of them that warmed his heart in depth. How lucky he was. Had wonderful Aunt Aethelflaeda been so blessed? It was a shame he had been too young to understand such emotional matters, though she had done her best training him, for which he felt eternal gratitude. It was she who had paved the way to his kingship. Now he sat firmly in the royal saddle and could only hope all the bloodletting had ended. Had it though?

He thought about putting Rannulf in his local witan and for when he travelled his realm. He was well into his twenties now, but only that. It was possible some of the witan

195

members in their forties would pull a face at this, but then he shrugged to himself. 'I am their king!" he said firmly. 'It is my word,' he told himself, and it was this that counted. He considered Rannulf could look after himself. He had grown into a powerful, strong man, topping his king by a good head with large hands capable of turning into flailing fists. He had not yet seen Rannulf engage in any fights but suspected he could if pushed too far. Somewhere in his unusual pedigree was good blood, which would always out in the end.

He rode back into his adored home, dismounted, handed his horse to a servant, saw his gesith copy and strode towards Cerdic's large and rather splendid place. He saw Edith come out and waved happily to her.

'I feel hungry, good lady wife!' Aethelstan stated hopefully and beamed at her.

Edith laughed and bowed her head a little out of respect for his rank. 'I've never known you anything else, sire!' she teased back. 'You know my routine. Wash and change if you fancy roast boar with all the trimmings,' she began, then seized the opportunity. 'Sire,' she said in such a grave tone of voice that Aethelstan felt a flutter of rare alarm. Her eyes were so serious. What had gone wrong? Why hadn't a courier been sent for him?

'It's my beloved,' Edith began in a low voice, making sure Cerdic was not around.

'Is he ill?' Now Aethelstan flinched. Surely

not his great friend?

'Not yet, but he will be if he keeps doing these long rides. They are simply too much for him now!' and Edith knew she had stated this before. 'You really must order him to stay at home!'

'Oh!' Aethelstan managed to get out. 'I agree with you completely, but short of tying him down . . .' he began, defending himself, but this time Edith was firmer.

'It's no good, sire. It has to stop. Now! Dead in its tracks!'

Aethelstan puffed his cheeks. She was quite right of course, but he didn't know what to do for once. 'I don't know what I can do, good lady wife,' he ended hopefully. 'You know how knuckle-headed your good man can be!'

Edith had to agree with him and she bit her lip, but had an idea. 'In that case if you can't stop him from riding to battle tell him I shall ride with him!' she pronounced.

'What!'

'I mean it, sire.'

He looked deep into serious eyes. She did indeed mean it. 'Very well,' he replied slowly. 'So be it, but the battles appear to have ended now. There is no reason at all why England cannot be at peace,' he prevaricated calmly. His martial instinct warned him this statement might be more wishful than factual, but it would get Edith off his back and he was so hungry. Roast boar? His nostrils twitched, picking up delightful aromas. 'Bath and change, good lady wife?' he asked hopefully.

'Oh, get on with you, sire. You know where to go and the women will have hot water for you!' she said and shooed him away with her hands, not in the slightest impressed with what he'd said. Men! Bloodthirsty lot!

With his stomach comfortably full and relishing Edith's ale, Aethelstan was not inclined to discuss business, though he could see both Cerdic and Ceorl itched to. 'In the morrow!' he told them, and waited for a tankard refill. That was another day and he was not going to spoil this lovely evening with his friends. He was going to permit himself the pleasure of getting just a bit drunk, but he was alert enough to see how Rannulf rationed his ale intake. He nodded with understanding and approval at him, and Rannulf threw him a wide grin of acknowledgement.

In the morning, once refreshed, and with surprisingly clear heads, the four of them gathered outside for business.

'Those churls rode back in last evening,' Cerdic said. 'I told both of them to hang about, as you wished to speak to them.'

'Right! To business!' Aethelstan announced firmly.

Ceorl carefully explained his thoughts in depth, while Cerdic, Rannulf and Aethelstan listened critically.

Aethelstan shook his head. 'I'd never have

thought of something like a simple belt. It's brilliant!'

Rannulf took over. He produced a small piece of parchment. 'See, sire!' he began and wrote. 'Note these two signs. This one means alert. The second is for danger. Only those of us present here will be able to read them and they can easily be taken for wear marks on the leather!'

'So they can!' Aethelstan breathed. 'Quite perfect!' he praised, and Ceorl went pink-cheeked with pleasure. 'Right! That's our code, and both men are to wear the belts. They'll wonder why though?'

Cerdic had that answer. 'Just say it's one of your idiosyncrasies. A royal wish or whatever!'

'In that case we'll all take to wearing similar belts,' Aethelstan told them. 'They've become a royal fetish or something to keep the tunic tidy! I'll start wearing one myself from now on, and the rest of you copy.'

'And we only take notice of the belt that carries the code!' Ceorl announced, feeling rather smug with himself. He made Aethelstan grin and the rest copied. It was rare to see Ceorl sit looking puffed-up with pride.

'Now bring those two churls over. I'll talk to them. Does anyone happen to know where Anlaf is?'

'The last we heard he was still in Dublin, and Olaf is there also,' Cerdic said. 'Can't do much damage that far away, especially after

Constantine's last beating.'

This made sense to all, but Aethelstan knew while Anlaf lived he would always be a troublemaker. A king had not been crowned anywhere who did not have to cope with such.

The two churls bowed their heads respectfully while Aethelstan eyed them in silence. He knew this type. Tough, rugged, with little education. Good allies. Bad foes. Rather like his naval captain Burhred, the identical stamp of man, the backbone of his country.

'I have a job. A very special job, but it is for volunteers only,' he began, and noted how both men threw each other a look and stiffened with interest. 'It will pay well from me or my treasury direct. It may be interesting. It could be utterly boring. How long it will last I cannot say, because I do not know myself. There may or may not be personal danger, which is why I do not issue any direct order to a man whose oath I have taken,' and he paused to let his words sink home and study their joint reaction. Did the father lead or was the young son impetuous and impatient to take that role?

'We're listening, sire!' they chorused together, which made him smile.

'You will each have to wear a special leather belt, either under or over your tunics!' he told them.

Now that had foxed them as their dual frowns showed. Aethelstan had reached the crux of the matter but wanted one more piece of information.

'Domestic ties either of you?'

They both shook their heads firmly. 'Just each other,' Aidan the father explained. 'We happen to like each other's company, strange as this may sound to some.'

'Belts, sire?' Edred the son asked with a puzzled frown.

Aethelstan snapped his fingers and Cerdic came forward to hand them over where Rannulf had carefully worked on both of them. They were perfectly plain black leather belts, quite utilitarian but strongly made, even if a little the worse for wear. The buckles were of plain steel, and the buckle's loop the same. He handed them over and both men studied them from end to end without understanding at all, which pleased Aethelstan, and Cerdic also gave a satisfied nod.

'They're good strong belts albeit on the plain side, but with marks on them,' Aidan said thoughtfully, then he threw the king a discerning look. 'Marks? But each belt has a different mark and . . .' he allowed his wits to work, then his eyes brightened with understanding. Edred was still baffled though.

'These different marks mean something, sire! They are not old knife gouges as I first thought! Nor have these marks come from being caught on obstructions like clothing when rock-climbing, which tears. They

201

mean . . .' and he halted to shake his head while Edred bent to see where his father pointed. Then he too realised.

'They carry a message, sire!' Aidan said softly. 'A personal message only for a king or his trusted adviser like a senior witan man!'

'Spot on!' Aethelstan said and waited. Did they want such a job? 'You would have to travel,' he warned them. 'You would need an occupation to explain your presence, like hunting! Remember, I said it might be incredibly boring and neither do I have the faintest idea of the timescale involved.'

Father and son looked at each other. Speech was often unnecessary between them because they could often be like twin brothers. They knew each other's minds in depth. They were a highly unusual pair.

'We are interested, sire.' Aidan said.

'Very much so!' Edred chimed in.

'I think I can guess, sire,' Aidan said slowly. 'Code marks to warn you about . . . ?' and he left the sentence hanging.

'Exactly. A message that may never come but with information I must have immediately if a certain situation arose.'

Now it was Edred's turn to be first off the mark. 'An invasion by an enemy, sire?' he guessed, then explained more. 'Constantine of the north. You have beaten him twice but don't trust him one bit. You are concerned about something that may happen in the future if he gets fresh allies?'

'Very correct indeed! Forewarned is very much forearmed,' Aethelstan confirmed dryly. 'The situation though may never arise, which is why I warn this task could turn out incredibly boring.'

The churls looked at each other and nodded together. 'We're on, sire! Even if it should stay peaceful and boring we can earn a good living as hunters and pelt-skinners. We are easily able to live off the land when it suits us, and in bad weather we can always find a dry roof on some estate,' Aidan smiled.

'Especially if we turn up with a deer's carcass to roast for a venison feast!' Edred chipped in.

'Splendid!' Aethelstan said and flashed a look at Cerdic, who had come prepared. He opened the purse attached to his own belt and produced four gold coins, which he gave to the king. Aethelstan took them and handed them over to the churls with gravity.

'I hold your oaths of loyalty to me only and I now pay you for a year's observations in advance. Make sure you are always well mounted and bring the correct belt if a situation arises. Cerdic here will go over this with you again and, of course, there must be total secrecy at all times. Not just for me but your sake too. Spies, when caught, are never treated leniently, so it might be prudent if you vanished now and again, anywhere, but always return to a set region.'

'Taking pelts to sell or barter,' Edred suggested, and Aidan nodded. 'So we must have a couple of pack horses for authenticity.'

Aethelstan nodded and walked from them. They were sufficiently worldly wise to know how to protect their cover. He had so many other duties but first there was the Edith problem. He flashed a look at Cerdic, who came back to join him in a stroll.

'Now that's sorted out we can move on to problem two. Edith!'

Cerdic was startled. 'Eh?'

Aethelstan related Edith's conversation and rigid tone of voice. 'I'm not fighting your good lady wife and, anyhow, she does have a point. You are too old now to be gadding about my kingdom on horses. We've had this conversation before, if you remember, but carts appear to be out so, good friend, the time has come for you to stay at home and hold my land for me here. Fight Edith? I'd prefer not!' and now his voice rang regally with firm order.

Cerdic scowled, then saw Edith's point. She would follow too, he knew, and that would never do. At least, he reminded himself, despite the clandestine arrangements just made, it would have to be a sorry state of affairs for there to be another battle. As to riding around with the king's court all over his land, he had no objection to avoiding these meetings. They were hard work and Rannulf would always attend and bring the news back with him or send a personal courier.

'I understand, sire. Edith on her personal warpath could even be dangerous, so yes, I'll consent to be the stay-at-home oldie.'

Later, he related the whole conversation to Ceorl, and Judith, sitting to one side, chewed her lip. Cerdic was not the only one getting too old. Ceorl was the same, but perhaps worse.

Last night when in bed she had wriggled, so she lay with her head on his chest and one ear flat, listening hard. She had not liked what she'd heard. His heart lacked regular beat—instead it was inclined to be erratic, which explained why some days his lips had the suggestion of a blue tinge.

She had digitalis in her medical pouch. First-year leaves picked and dried naturally, and second years treated the same, which inclined to be stronger, but kept in another packet. She had discovered Ceorl was apt to be a fastidious eater, and it had proved difficult to make him take an infusion to strengthen his heart. She would not argue with him because she knew increased emotional tension would only exacerbate his condition. She now realised it was this about him that gave her sad feelings, so why did she also have this for the king? He was so fit, powerful and healthy. Was this the first time her natural instinct was about to play tricks with her? One thing was sure. This wonderful, kind man was never going to make old bones. Where did this then leave her?

Judith thought about where she lived and her current domestic life. It was not to her taste and she knew when the inevitable happened she would give in and yield to her natural spirit, which now craved strongly for her old free, wandering life. It was true, she would end up old and alone, somewhere remote and waiting to die, as had happened to the old mother, but was it really such a terrible way to go? Animals did not make a fuss, they accepted it in silence and with fortitude. In so many ways, although she had a good brain, she was simply just another two-legged animal. Osburga would miss her, but only for a little while. She had a good man also, and there were her children now. She was permanent in this region and happily settled down. She would miss her personal friendship but only for a short while, and she would always have her memories.

Also Judith kept getting prods from her instinct. There had been the last great battle, but if this was the final one, why did she keep getting feelings of always having to be ready? What was on the horizon that she was not yet privy to? Something momentous and dreadful. All she could do was wait for something to happen, then follow her natural instinct.

TWELVE

Aethelstan gave a grunt of satisfaction. This year was ending well. He had commenced prowling his realm, listening to matters of law and justice. Now he was heading down to Cirencester for another council meeting, where he expected Constantine to be present. He had found that after a while and a few drinks his old enemy could even become affable, which made life easier. He was realistic enough to accept there could never be a proper friendship with Constantine, unlike the camaraderie he enjoyed with his old friends down in Mercia, even if they were of lower rank.

He allowed gentle familiarity and made sure Constantine mixed with the other sub-kings in a free and easy way, all of which helped to make a good atmosphere. Not that he trusted him yet, but he was thankful he had the two churls keeping a discreet eye on his northern realm.

He brought Constantine's son with him, teaching him as he travelled, as he had been taught. He fostered other young people and found time to take an interest in their training and education. Constantine was impressed with this smart, well-mannered son, whose tutors were delighted with his progress.

'Now you must admit he's fine,' Aethelstan told him. 'Happy with the other youngsters, and you know anyhow you would have sent him away for his education!'

Constantine nodded but was still unhappy at his son being with this king, but there was nothing he could do about the situation. He was thankful he still had an older son, just about a man, who gave promise of being a fine warrior in his own right. So he allowed himself to play along, but, at the same time, could not help but be impressed by the many young people fostered by Aethelstan at his court.

One of Aethelstan's sisters brought her son Louis to shelter and learn at his court when her husband Charles was captured and imprisoned. He also had Alan of Brittany and the son of Harald of Norway—all of them thriving and a credit to Aethelstan. Constantine was also enormously impressed by the never-ending stream of worldly scholars who came to learn and expand their education—so many races and nationalities they left Constantine feeling isolated and even humble. Among them was the Icelandic Egill Skallagrimsson. What impressed him even more was the fact that Aethelstan had time to talk to everyone, young or adult, and even get involved in geometric puzzles. Somehow this was all difficult to assimilate, yet always at the back of his mind was the knowledge this man had bested him twice and he was now only a sub-king, which was a permanent, festering sore, and quite humiliating. He was also very conscious of his age. In two years, in 937, he would be sixty, and it was unlikely he would live much longer after that. But Aethelstan? He still brimmed with youth, fitness and astonishing health and strength. Why had he not married? Why no direct heir? Surely he was not one of—them? Impossible!

He would have been aghast to learn Aethelstan read his mind from his body language and sheer astute deduction.

'I have no need to make an heir,' Aethelstan told him bluntly at one meeting. 'I have an excellent half brother who thinks just like me. In about a year he will be with me as an adult and we shall be joint rulers. We are of the same blood, and if it is destined for me to go early, he becomes King. I have this in my will, which is held by Mother Church.'

Constantine picked up the message loud and clear but refrained from comment. 'I too have another son, probably the same age as your brother,' he replied quietly. Just as well to let him know that although old he too was not alone.

They eyed one another in silence. It was as if they were two dogs, unsure of who was going to grab the bone as they warily circled watching each other, ready to snap then fight.

Aethelstan let the matter drop and turned his attention to a more charming guest. He knew though he must let his hostage return to his mother. It was not the boy's fault his father was so stupid and intractable. But trust him he never would.

He had Constantine with him at court then passed his hostage back, and at the same time invited Constantine to Christ's Mass that December, which the Welsh sub-kings would attend. Constantine did not turn up, and his absence shrieked louder than any words. 'So be it,' Aethelstan told himself. Later on in that year, when his travels brought him back to his second favourite home after Malmesbury, Cerdic alerted him:

'The two churls have ridden in, sire. They wish to speak to you.'

Aethelstan saw them as soon as he could. 'News?' he asked them as they stood before him, still in travel-stained clothes.

Aidan handed him one belt from around his waist. 'We had no idea whether we would see you in person, sire, but it is this mark!' and he displayed the open belt in his hands and pointed.

'The alert!' he said with a grunt. 'What's going on in that area?'

Aidan shook his head. It had been a long ride but they had made the excuse of a trading trip laden with pelts.

'We don't really know, sire, but there has been more activity than usual, with couriers and messengers riding all over the region, especially heading westwards,' Edred said and shook his head. 'We can neither of us work it out. The area seems to be peaceful but . . .' and he allowed the sentence to hang.

'You've done very well,' Aethelstan praised. This was food for thought indeed. 'Now go and get cleaned up. The good lady wife here is most particular about dress and cleanliness at her table, but it will be worth the effort for her food, which is excellent!'

When they had gone he discussed this news with Cerdic. 'He's up to no good again,' Cerdic muttered thoughtfully. 'Does he never learn? Is he so obtuse?'

'I agree with your logic,' Aethelstan replied slowly. 'Obtuse perhaps, or being stirred up for action by others who are using him, and he's too dim to see it!'

'Your wishes, sire?'

'Keep on exactly as of now but make sure I can always be reached in a hurry. I will dictate a letter to go to Burhred, to give him what facts we have plus our suspicions. There is going to be another fight and this time both Constantine and his fighting son must be taken out. He simply causes far too much trouble too often. You were right. I should not have let my hostage of the younger son go. I made a grave error. I let my heart rule my head for once,' and he pulled a face at himself. 'I doubt wonderful Aunt Aethelflaeda would have done this. It's done now but our need for up-to-date information is very vital indeed. Pay those two churls well. Be generous, because without them up there we might be taken by surprise. Do you think we have any spies among us or in my court?'

Cerdic considered. 'I don't think so,' he replied after a little thought. 'The gesith between them know all of the men, especially strangers who wander in to give their oaths.'

'Keep the men fit and ready for anything, but also make sure the weapons-maker is flat out. We must have ample weapons, especially throwing spears and hacking javelins. Get some sound shields made, enough for everyone. And of course if there should be another battle you DO NOT attend. That is a very direct order, good friend. I do not fancy going to war against your wife! No way!'

'It would be the first time . . .' Cerdic began with a deep grumble.

'Tough, old friend!' Aethelstan barked and meant it. 'Look at Ceorl. He has also aged but stays at home without making any fuss about it!'

'I don't like this at all!' Cerdic insisted upon having the final word, but the king simply smiled at his chagrin.

'You'll get over it,' he replied a little uncharitably. 'Can you tell me honestly that the thought of many miles in the saddle appeals to you now?'

Cerdic gave him a rueful look. 'You win,

212

sire. The very idea makes me baulk!' he admitted. 'No man likes to think he's become that aged though!'

Aethelstan was delighted he had won without a sulking uproar, and at how pleased Edith would be. His next task now was to reflect upon the map of his realm. In all his many journeys around his kingdom he had always followed his aunt's advice in meticulous detail.

'Know your realm,' she had advised. 'Don't ride around with your eyes half shut! Study all in depth. Is this region suitable for a battle? Is there water for thirsty warriors? Remember what I told you about the debacle of Dyrham. Those three British kings should have won hands down, as they had such a huge army against the Saxons, but they were complacent, short-sighted and too cocky. Who finds plenty of water on high ground? They deserved to lose as they did!'

He nodded sagely as he sat in his chamber and studied a map drawn up by Ceorl. It needed detail filling in but there were few regions he had failed to visit, and with his excellent memory he had no trouble in shutting his eyes and seeing them in his mind.

It was blindingly obvious Constantine was up to no good again. Twice he had gone to his battlefield, but not a third time. He would choose to suit himself. He looked at the rivers Severn and Humber. Such wide, powerful waterways were pure roads, so precautions must be taken for both to be guarded. He did not like splitting his naval forces, but he would write to Burhred and explain the problem, which might arise in the not-so-distant future. As an old mercenary Burhred, who had demonstrated he was a fine naval man, would instantly understand potential problems. Right now each river was on an opposing flank, both unguarded and dangerous.

He planned to move on again to London to speak with his witan there about monies. What was the exact state of his treasury? This would make an excellent place in which to meet Burhred to explain his current thinking. That cunning old wolf might even have ideas that he had overlooked. 'Unlikely,' he told himself, but *he* would never fall victim to complacency and cockiness.

It would be strange without reliable Cerdic's presence, but Rannulf, with his fast writing, would keep his old friend informed. Ceorl too would be missed desperately but both were realistic enough to understand the years were to blame. Their spirits were still so willing but their flesh had now cried that enough was more than enough.

He rode off with his gesith in the morning, head filled with his plans. Cerdic's eyes had been reproachful, while those of Edith had shone with approval. Osburga had nothing to say to him, her whole attention concentrated on her darling Rannulf, while Judith was her usual silent self. Then Aethelstan dismissed them from his mind to concentrate on matters in hand.

Judith knew her instincts were at full stretch. She would see her king again, of that she was sure, yet why did she feel sadness for him as well? He was the very picture of masculine health, vigour and strength. She was very well aware that good healer as she had become, she and others of her kind were limited in what they could do, even with their wonderful medicinal plants. The blood was of critical importance to life, and she had some understanding of its circulation. Whenever she killed game she would always skin then dissect it, as old mother had taught her, so she had a first-class understanding of what happened in the body, though as to blood itself—did it too get ill? How? What happened to it? What could be done—if anything? Did a person with ailing blood give symptoms? What were they? There was so much she yearned to learn. What she was sure of was heart conditions, and that applied to Ceorl.

He had aged even faster than Cerdic who was, if anything, a little older than he was. One late evening he sat down by her side and held her in his arms.

'I suspect I don't have long to go,' he said out of the blue.

She was startled. 'What on earth makes you

say that?'

Ceorl explained. 'Everything is such hard work now. I tire far more easily than I should. Just like my old father. I can see him now. He died in his sleep, so peaceful, so don't you be shocked one morning—'

'Ceorl!' she protested, even though she knew he was correct.

He shook his head. 'But if you do nothing else worthwhile in your life, my time with you has been so incredibly happy. Always remember that!'

Judith had no words. She would not insult his intelligence with lies. Now this had come into the open she knew she must consider herself when alone. There was going to be another battle. Her instinct told her so without being privy to special information. She and her kind would be needed again. Osburga was certainly out, so she realised she must seek for her own acolyte. Her knowledge could not be allowed to die with her. Somewhere, just waiting to be discovered, would be a young, lonely female with no proper place in the life of a vil. Like the way the old mother had found her. Words had been unnecessary, once their eyes had met. She could distinctly remember grabbing a small backpack and following. Those days were long gone, with little remembered except the old mother. Now *she* had moved into that category.

She knew she was self-sufficient in living

off the land, and could even construct a reasonable shelter in the winter months. There would be no people around until her skills were required, and no horses. It would be back to walking as and where she fancied. A couple of spears with short shafts, a small shield that could double as a mixing platter. Two very good knives from her belt, and even, perhaps, a small javelin. A slingshot could also be carried for little game, and small pebbles for ammunition. She would need nothing else except flints to make fire and two drinking mugs. All easily carried, of little weight. Suddenly her heart throbbed with anticipation. How she had missed her roving life! She had taken in the old mother's words, tried this life of luxury, but her spirit was restless. The old mother had been so wise. Had she gently pushed her into this life to make a pointed comparison, with a final decision being hers and hers alone? Osburga and the rest of these friends were welcome to their comfortable homes. She felt alien in such. She would copy the old mother and in the middle of the night quietly walk away from it all. Just vanish until she was needed, by injured and maimed warriors somewhere, some place, some time, all yet unknown to her, except it was as inevitable as day followed night.

Ceorl died that night. Judith awoke with the dawn and knew instantly. He lay stiff in *rigor mortis* but on his face was an expression

217

of great peace and calm. For the first time in her adult life the tears flooded. He had been so good and kind. He had worshipped her and she knew, never again, would any other human being have such genuine affection for her. She felt humbled and took time to collect herself before standing and calling to Rannulf. He was now the master of the house, and she must prepare to go.

Cerdic could hardly take it in, and Edith grieved with him. Osburga's tears flowed copiously, then she turned to Judith with a speculative look.

'I know,' she said in a quiet sorrowful voice. 'You will also go now and I look upon you as my big sister!'

Judith had no reply, rather surprised at Osburga's words and her prescience. There was nothing to say. She was astonished Osburga had worked this out so fast, so obviously this had been something always there in the younger girl's mind. She just gave her gentle smile of acknowledgement but said not one word.

'The king must be told!' Cerdic said turning to Rannulf. 'Write and tell him while I find a fast courier. He's in the London area so should not be too difficult to locate, unless he's already moved northwards again!'

*   *   *

Aethelstan eyed Burhred as they drank ale by the side of one of the wharves of the Thames.

'So you see, I've nothing to go on but . . .' he tapped his nose. 'Something is starting to smell!'

Burhred liked him both as a king and as a man. In another time and place he knew they would have made a good pair of fighting mercenary brothers.

'Looting been good?' Aethelstan asked with a twinkle in both eyes.

'Most profitable, sire. At this rate I'll be starting to get rich and will have to put money on deposit with your treasury! Or wend my way to York and speak to a Jew and see what he will offer. Where money deposits are concerned they can't really be beaten, can they?' Burhred chuckled then became serious as to the king's current state of affairs, which was running and ruling England. 'Those rivers are the weak point on your two flanks,' he agreed.

'They need to be patrolled constantly now, and certainly until I learn which way the wind is going to blow from . . .' and Aethelstan nodded to the north then west.

Burhred agreed. 'Split the navy then. That's the only sensible answer! I have a good man to captain one flank. The other I'll take myself, of course!'

'Which?'

Burhred pondered. 'Stands to reason the

Severn is the more dangerous river to you, sire, so I'll go there!'

'Good man!' and Aethelstan was delighted. By doing this his flanks would be fully protected, come what may. He would deal with the land portion himself. There was a sudden hustle and bustle among his personal guards and both he and Burhred went on alert.

'Now what is it?' Aethelstan said with a low groan. It could only be trouble of course, for someone to wish to interrupt him.

Burhred moved by his side, his hand ready to whip out a javelin, then the guards let a man through. He was obviously hot and bothered.

'Sire,' he cried with relief. 'I've found you!' and he handed over two objects. One was a letter sealed with Cerdic's sign, the second was a rather worn leather belt. Aethelstan grabbed this first and eyed it carefully. Yes! There it was. The agreed sign for danger.

'How did you get this belt!' Aethelstan barked.

'It came in with two men, sire. Lord Cerdic was having this letter written and told me to get it and this belt to you as fast as possible.'

'A father-and-son pair?'

The messenger frowned. 'I didn't stop to ask, sire, but, come to think of it, there was some resemblance.'

Aethelstan turned to Burhred who stood puzzled. 'I must get back to Mercia as quickly as possible,' and he broke the seal and swiftly read Cerdic's short note and pulled a face. 'Someone has died for whom I've always had the greatest respect, regard and affection. Gesith! We ride to Mercia! Get fresh, strong horses. We ride right away,' and he turned back to Burhred. 'I'll leave all naval matters in your hands but . . .' and he waved the belt. 'It has happened. My nose has not let me down after all! I'll see you're kept informed. Cerdic is a stay-at-home now. He can handle the messengers. Too old to go to battle though, and he's not best pleased!' he grinned.

Burhred had to smile also. 'And I'd be just the same, sire!'

'Mount up. Ride!' Aethelstan shouted once more, and there was a scramble onto saddles, then with a rumble of hooves the king departed at a fast pace. 'He won't be able to keep up that pace for long without foundering horses,' Burhred told himself. Perhaps the sea and ships had a definite advantage after all.

*   *   *

Cerdic and Rannulf took over. Judith was amazed at how distraught Ceorl's death had left her. She could not halt the cascade of tears. It was sad their time together had not been longer, then she took herself to task. Who was it who had said, 'Better to have loved and lost than never loved at all'? Now she must plan and arrange the life still available

221

to her. She knew Cerdic had sent for the king, just as her natural instinct warned her services were going to be needed.

It was Cerdic who arranged for the coffin and short funeral service, and Ceorl was interred in his own land at one corner. His own heart was heavy with disbelief and he turned to Judith.

'Did you suspect or know?' he asked her.

She nodded. 'There was nothing I could really do. Ceorl was difficult with all medicines and he also knew his time was up,' and she related their last conversation. 'He just took after his father.'

There were cries of alarm from the sentries and Cerdic grabbed a spear, then lowered it. Only one person could ride at that pace given the circumstances. Aidan and Edred also lowered their weapons. They had dug the grave and waited, like all of them, for the king.

Aethelstan dismounted, slowly for him. It had been a fast ride and they had left a trail of exhausted horses behind them.

'I can hardly believe it!' he said heavily. 'I'll miss him very much!'

'Like all of us, sire,' and Cerdic passed on Judith's words. 'Now, sire, the two churls. Here, you two!'

Aethelstan faced them. 'Right. What's going on?'

As usual Aidan spoke for both of them. 'It's war again, sire. Constantine and some other of the Scots kings who signed the Treaty of Penrith have joined forces with Anlaf and Olaf, who have sailed over with a huge army. Within a couple of weeks we heard they plan to invade you.'

'Is that so?' Aethelstan grated, but not in the least surprised. Constantine had been building up for his two previous defeats. Anlaf would do anything to beat and kill the King of England. This had obviously been planned since he released his hostage—his one grave mistake, or was it? Constantine and his allies would never give up until they were killed. So did it matter about letting the young hostage go? Better to have this out in the open, once and for all. He turned to Cerdic. 'Get my brother Edmund at once!' he ordered, his mind racing. His flanks were protected on the rivers. If the enemy tried a land invasion from those places they were in for an awful shock. So let them invade. It was now his turn to pick the battlefield, and he stood, eyes closed, visualising the map of his realm.

The enemy had to come over the high land of Northumbria, but he would pick a small place he well remembered called Brunanburh. There was good flat land around and the enemy would have to march there with weapons and food. All so tiring, while he could take his time. They would also be forced to erect defences hastily, which would be more tiring for men who had marched long and hard. Let them get there first. They could even go ahead and quickly dig a ditch and erect a fence, but shelter it would not be for them. They might guess his tactics with a hastily erected defensive structure, but it would be impossible for them to ring the whole area. This would be a case for a frontal assault as well as flanking ones. The enemy must be softened up first. 'Copy the Romans,' Aethelstan reminded himself. A discharge of weapons through the air to fall on those behind the front ranks. Nothing panicked men more than when those in the front suddenly realised their rear was undefended.

He called Cerdic to him, and with Oswald and Egbert started to explain. They listened to him intently and mulled it over.

'Get a patrol off as quickly as possible, to move all the inhabitants from that vil as well as their livestock. Take carts and move them quickly to safety.'

'The enemy will know where you intend to stand, sire!' Cerdic pointed out. 'Is this wise?'

Aethelstan nodded. 'Let them. They can waste valuable time and men's energy in digging a trench and erecting a heavy fence. We shall end up going around at the instant their frontal shields break, as they will. I want men from all my sub-kings and continental brothers-in-law and any mercenaries around who are eager for loot. My army this time must be quite massive. They may think they can muster fighting men but I want them to look with awe at my numbers, so messages off everywhere. Get Rannulf writing and keep plenty of fast couriers available.'

'They have to ship over from Dublin,' Cerdic murmured thoughtfully. 'You say our two rivers have the navy lying in wait. It might take just a little while for men to come from the continent though!'

'I think not!' and Aethelstan threw him a rogue's smile. 'I've suspected this for a very long time, and warned my brothers-in-law to come quickly when I send. They will because they all adore their wives, my lovely sisters! I suspect men have been gathered for a while near their ports. The enemy will have his own spies out. Let him see the vil of Brunanburh be cleared and make his own deductions. It would suit me for them to dig in. Battles are rarely won from static positions, and it is always better to be offensive than defensive!'

His small witan nodded in agreement. There was much to organise, but they were efficient and approved the king's plan. A frontal assault after a discharge of weapons to the enemy's rear, then reserves to attack from left and right. There would be no stopping— the men would be encouraged to fight on in groups for mutual defence. The reserves must be nicely balanced in number. Most of all, they must have adequate weapons available.

'Discharge of spears or javelins, sire?'

'Both!' Aethelstan told them bluntly. 'Let the spears go over first, then a wave of javelins.'

That made sense to all of them. They broke up and hurried away, as there was much more to do.

Aethelstan was satisfied. He turned and saw that Judith was watching. He smiled at her, walked forward and grasped her hands. 'You will be going now, won't you?' he asked in a soft voice.

Judith simply nodded. Words were unnecessary. She had collected all she would need and planned to slip off in the middle of the night. It was dry and she would be miles away by dawn. Her life here was ended.

'Do you want a horse?' Aethelstan asked, and understood when she shook her head. He would see her again, and he knew where.

THIRTEEN

Aethelstan sat on his horse and gazed thoughtfully at what was facing him. He was unimpressed. 'See!' he said and pointed. 'Once I cleared that vil they worked it out and are now frantically busy building frontal defences.'

'Should we stop them, brother?' Edmund asked uncertainly. This was his first experience of the real thing. He knew he was well trained and proud of what he was, confident at what he could do, but facing this vast horde was another matter.

'No. I want them to carry on. No attack yet. I want all their men nice and exhausted. Digging a deep ditch and erecting a stout fence uses up a lot of strength. Apart from that, they have to get their materials here and all must be carried. Those men are using energy better kept for battle. Look at our men! Rested. Well fed and quite refreshed. It's true they're chomping at the bit to sail forward in all their bloodlust, but they *are* highly disciplined. They will not move until they have the word. Each sector has a strong man in charge, who knows my wishes to the final detail. And another advantage we have that has not yet hit them . . .' and he paused and eyed his brother, for whom he had great affection.

He had grown into a splendid man even if still only eighteen. He was tall, taller than Aethelstan, and there was not an ounce of fat on him. Plenty of lean, hard muscle from constant exercise and martial training. He was so handsome too. It was not going to take long for the ladies' eyes to sparkle whenever he appeared.

'What is that?' Edmund asked.

'We have one overall leader. Me! The enemy have too many kings and others wishing to lead. It won't take much for them to fall out. Divide and rule has always been a

227

great policy!' Aethelstan chuckled. 'There's Constantine and his favourite adult son, and the other sub-kings who have reneged on the Treaty of Penrith. There is Anlaf, a constant thorn in my side, who has joined in with Olaf. We have sub-kings on our side who have sworn to follow my orders. Mercenaries have appeared and also vowed the same, as well as warriors from the continent. All told, the same. Not one movement until I give the word, and my plan is to be followed to the letter. They had a good moon last night and worked right through, so the enemy should be tired. We now have dawn, the sun is coming up, so it's time to get our mail on. I think this may well turn into a long day!'

'Let's make sure I have it straight,' Edmund said. 'This is all very new to me, brother, through no fault of mine.'

'We will have the frontal attack with thrown weapons—only then will the flanks move in. You take the right. I'll have the left. Once we've circumnavigated their ditch and fence we join and move forward as one. To be effective their defences should have been very long, but they've not had the time, and we will move off on horseback, then fight on foot,' Aethelstan explained.

Edmund frowned. 'But the frontal attack ...?'

'Easy! The first man bends, makes a back for the second to climb, and the third passes

228

him weapons!' Aethelstan went on: 'After there has been a mass discharge of spears, to thin out their crowded back ranks, a good hail of javelins will fall much shorter and take out even more. Then our front rank can rampage faster.'

'Well!' Edmund said with glowing eyes. He turned and looked at an enormous mass of warriors, all standing impatiently waiting for the king's signal. He had never seen so many men in all his life, and his awed expression showed this.

'It will be the same with our enemy,' Aethelstan confirmed, 'so we use shock tactics, ones I've never used before, so they'll be unprepared. They will expect us to come around their flanks, so it will be a head-on charge on foot. Make sure you don't get ahead of your bodyguard,' he warned. 'Watch from your periphery vision at all times. In our chain mail we will stand out as the leaders, and the determined ones will die in trying to take us out.'

Aethelstan felt a pang of doubt. A real battle was not the best teaching ground. Was he asking too much of his young brother? One look at Edmund's set jaw and glowing eyes reassured him. They both carried Alfred and Aethelflaeda's blood and spirit.

Aethelstan signalled and their chain mail and helmets were brought to them. 'We can't expect the men to wait much longer. It only needs one hothead and they'll surge forward. They can barely stand still now,' he grunted as they both dived into their mail. They settled their helmets and buckled their scabbards onto their belts.

They both saw men were edging forward impatiently, and Aethelstan waved, then grabbed Edmund and dragged him sideways to two horses. It was a tidal wave of warriors, who had practised. Each man knew what to do. A wave of spears was thrown, with another as the first was still in flight—then a third. Immediately there were cries from the far side of the barrier, then came three flights of javelins. Without a spear's long shaft these would fall much shorter and wound men close to the barrier. The men surged again, each front man dropping to his knee to make a back. A second climbed on his living platform, while a third handed the warrior the weapon of his choice.

There were massive cries of enemy pain at this unexpected fusillade of death, which hurtled into them from the sky. Then Aethelstan's men were up, over the barrier, jumping the ditch and scrambling forward with slashing weapons, in an uncontrollable wave of murderous bloodlust.

'Ride!' Aethelstan bellowed, and Edmund mounted, spun his horse aside, drew and waved his sword and led another roaring charge aside. Each man, yearning to kill, followed his trusted leader into battle on both flanks.

Aethelstan dismounted at the edge of the enemy barricade, and with his men pressing eagerly behind, and his gesith strung out on both sides, he waded into men who met him with equal passion. The noise was a cacophony of dreadful sounds as battle-hardened warriors received devastating blows, driving them to scream out their agonies. Aethelstan plunged with his sword, slashing and stabbing, parrying similar blows with adroit use of his shield and by ducking under others. It was all vicious action, with quarter neither asked nor given. It was simply kill or be killed, and a man wearing chain mail, with the royal sword, became everyone's desired target. His gesith were hard-pressed, but Aethelstan pounded ever onwards, cleaving a path to his front, leaving bodies in his wake.

His men followed his lead and the battle waged hot and furious with more warriors pouring forwards to fill in the gaps. Even Aethelstan, with his strength and fitness, was soon sweating. His chain mail was liberally covered with others' blood. A few javelins managed to stab between the mail links, but his leather undercoat turned away their points, though his trunk soon began to ache with the bruising.

Aethelstan fought on. He paused only once, for three heartbeats, to throw a look to his right, where he saw the flash of Edmund's mail. So far so good, but now to join up the two flanks.

'To the right!' he roared, wondering if he'd been heard, the din was so shocking with cries of agony everywhere. He started to slash his way to the right, sword flashing, covered in blood, never still. Once it found a target he aimed for another. Up and down, left and right, stab and slash remorselessly. His men intelligently understood his aim and crowded with him, a heaving body of angry warriors, bloodlust still at fever pitch.

Edmund flashed a look to his left and understood. 'To the left!' he bellowed. 'Join up with the king!'

Behind them was bloody mayhem. The earth was saturated with blood, hacked-off limbs and men rolling and crying in their agonies. Those who had succeeded at their frontal attempt now poured forth to join in the general melee. For a few heartbeats it was difficult to know who was friend or foe, but a man's action and aim soon solved such a small conundrum.

Then brother met brother, grinned, turned and slashed forward together, their men crowding with them. Aethelstan flashed a look at the sky. They seemed to have been fighting forever. Certainly time had passed remarkably quickly. The brothers drove forwards, and now the enemy had to start and backtrack against this ferocious assault of lethal weaponry. But there was no letup. They were chopped down as they tried to retreat or turn, many dying, others writhing on the red earth in the extremes of agonising pain.

'Keep at them!' Aethelstan roared and chopped another man's neck, so that his head hung by threads of skin and muscle. 'Attack!' Edmund echoed. The men followed these remarkable brothers, imitating them, though some were starting to tire, yet no man would give up until the king's sword was at rest.

Aethelstan drove himself onwards, though now his body cried for respite. Edmund did likewise. So did their men. 'Keep at it!' Aethelstan bellowed again. His right arm ached from wielding his sword, while his left quivered from the strain of manipulating the heavy, life-saving shield, and still Aethelstan fought ever onwards, with Edmund at his right hand.

Now the enemy did start to crack with a vengeance. They wanted to flee from these insane Englishmen. Could nothing stop them? They had so many dead and injured but kept advancing in hordes intent on one thing only, killing.

Then they broke almost in unison. They turned to flee. To their rear were ships to get them away from these madmen, but they had to reach them first. They were seemingly far away to these exhausted, bewildered and beaten warriors. They would have to fight their way to them, and that was miles, surely?

Aethelstan threw another look at the sky to calculate the passage of time. 'They're breaking, brother! But still go after them. Kill them on their ships if necessary!'

It had been an enormously long day, and soon evening would arrive. Aethelstan frowned, puzzled, as a horseman cantered up.

'What do you think you're doing here?' he rasped. 'Your place is safe at the rear. Scribes don't fight!'

Rannulf saw his king was more than a little testy, and when he looked around he understood. Aethelstan was covered in blood from helmet to boots, but obviously it wasn't his.

'Sire, I arranged for two stags to be caught, butchered and roasted for the men. They must be so hungry!' he hastened to explain.

Aethelstan felt his mouth fill with saliva. So was he. 'Where are they then?'

Rannulf swung in the saddle and pointed. 'Coming right now, sire. I thought you'd all want to eat, and water is on its way as well.'

'Smart work, scribe!' Aethelstan complimented, his good temper returning. This would hearten the men, though two stags would not go far—but better than nothing. They could then resume hounding the enemy, making his life hell on earth.

Rannulf read his mind. 'There's more

coming, sire. I arranged for some gerburs to come with us, and they've been busy making a kind of pottage in a cauldron. It's being driven up right now, so there should be some food for everyone, provided they don't pig it. Here it comes now!'

Aethelstan and Edmund spun round as a ramshackle small cart lumbered up, driven by one man.

'You!' Aethelstan gasped. 'You're leading my navy! Doesn't anyone follow orders!'

Burhred went red-cheeked. He had been very unsure of the enterprise when grabbed by this bossy scribe.

'Someone competent is in charge, sire. You couldn't expect me to keep away from battle, could you really?' he asked, placating.

Aethelstan let out a disparaging snort but was also amused, though he didn't let this show. 'Battle or loot?' he rasped.

The king turned to his brother. 'This is Burhred, born to fight and loot. Better for us than against,' he ended, and had to grin as relief flooded the hard-bitten warrior's face. 'Very well. The pair of you get as many men fed as possible so we can move on through the night. No stopping. The fight continues. It should be a cloudless night with a decent moon for us to continue fighting, and to get me and my brother mounted again!'

Rannulf sprang into action, as did Burhred. Already the nearest warriors had smelt the food and were clustering hopefully. Edmund looked at his brother and licked his own lips.

'The fighters first. We shall just take a tiny snack!' Aethelstan explained, and pulling out his dagger chopped two medium size pieces of venison for them both. They chomped slowly, to make the food last, while men gathered around them, where Burhred lined them up in a rough-and-ready queue.

'When you men have had something to eat, get a drink of water—then move out of the way and send others back!' Aethelstan ordered strongly. 'This fight has not finished!'

Rannulf cantered back, leading two horses, and the brothers mounted, each sheathing his sword temporarily. They walked onwards, and now the slaughter was horrific. Bodies lay sprawled as far as their eyes could see, intermingled with the maimed and wounded. Already medicine women had appeared from somewhere and were doing what they could.

Aethelstan turned to his gesith, sadly reduced in number, which made him wince. He shouted and gesticulated. 'Two men with javelins go with these medicine women. You know what to do when they signal!' he rasped, and pulled a face. Much better a sudden death than a lingering misery. There was a limit to what medicine women could do, skilled as they might be. He frowned as he looked to his left, then walked his horse forward slowly.

'Judith!' he said gently. 'You are indeed

236

needed.' He eyed her companion with frank curiosity. She was so young, barely more than a girl, and she walked dragging one foot.

Judith stepped forward and spoke in a low voice. 'My new acolyte, sire. Not wanted in her vil because of the clubfoot. She was leading a miserable life. I just signalled and she followed without hesitation. She has potential,' she confided softly. 'Her name is Alice. I have her with me, just as I was found years ago. History just repeating itself.'

Aethelstan nodded. The girl was too shy even to look at him, but he had faith in Judith's wisdom. 'The battle is going on through the night,' he explained. 'I intend to drive them back to their ships, and any who argue will die.'

Judith nodded. This she already knew, and yet again wondered why she felt some sadness in her heart for this splendid young king. She took a frank look at his brother and was likewise impressed, so why, suddenly, did this weird sadness encompass him too? She pushed these feelings into the back of her mind. One day her natural instinct would supply the answer. Until then, she would have to wait.

'These men come with you for when . . .' and Aethelstan did not bother to finish the sentence. Judith understood, and he swung his horse aside to walk forward, eyes everywhere, highly alert, just in case some dying warrior decided to try and take him out at this stage of the battle, in pure revenge. 'Be on your guard now!' But Edmund had already worked that one out.

Their horses did not like the smell of so much blood, or the bedlam, so they rode tight-reined, sitting securely, braced for sudden plunges from their upset mounts.

Aethelstan went first, observing all, estimating the numbers dead or soon to die. This was the biggest battle he had fought. It had gone on for so many long hours and was not finalised yet. He guessed it was probably the greatest battle ever fought on his beloved English soil.

Edmund pointed to one side and Aethelstan caught his breath. He knew that grey head. He recognised the posture. They walked up, then merely sat and stared. Aethelstan's expression was hard, unrelenting.

Constantine cried like a girl. The tears flooded down his dirty cheeks as he held the bloodied, chopped-up body in his arms. 'My son! My beloved son!'

'You only have yourself to blame,' Aethelstan shot back at him, in a deep growl of anger. He waved a hand. 'You are responsible for all these men too. I wonder you'll ever be able to sleep at nights. You are a very stupid old man, who never learns, and who breaks treaties and his oath to me as Senior King. I am within my rights to kill you here and now, but I won't. I'll let you suffer, you stupid, bigoted, useless old fool. You have sullied your name for all time. Now get yourself and him,' he nodded at the body, 'off my kingdom, before I change my mind and run you through myself. GET!' he raged.

Edmund was startled at the king's change of mood, to one of pure hatred. Later on, he knew his brother would explain, but he just sat silently now, shocked at this unusual bile from his brother.

Constantine was also horrified and frightened. He lurched erect, trying to hold his son's bleeding, lacerated body, until one of his fleeing men took pity on him and helped. The brothers watched them retreat, and Aethelstan let out a deep breath.

'He has finished himself. The tragedy is so many men have had to die because of him!' Aethelstan reflected.

Edmund shook his head. This was one day in his life he would never forget. Then five more riders arrived.

'Sire, you shouldn't be out here without us!' Hoel cried in agitation, as the reduced gesith formed a semi-circle round the royal brothers.

Aethelstan understood their concern. 'We've been careful and alert to that dying idiot! Now, eyes open. I want one man for myself. Anlaf! I have a personal score to settle with him. If we find him no man will meddle. It will be between me and him. Ask around. See if any warrior knows where he might be, but

239

don't kill him. He is my prey, and mine alone!'

They did this and always the answer was the same. 'The last anyone saw of him he was fleeing as fast as he could to get a ship to take him back to Dublin!' Hoel called over after talking to a dying man, then waved for a medicine woman.

Aethelstan calculated. The distance to any ship was still fairly great, but there were many routes over rough, high moorland. Wherever he looked he saw men putting as great a distance as possible between the English devil king and safety. 'Harry them! Hound them!' was Aethelstan's command, though even he was starting to tire. He yearned to get out of his armour, to get cleaned up, eat more then sleep, and he guessed Edmund felt the same. He had done wonderfully well for such a young man at his first battle.

Gradually Aethelstan's pace eased. He was so fatigued he had begun to slop around in his saddle. Giving a deep sigh he threw a look at Edmund. 'I think it's time we called it a day,' he admitted, for which his brother was truly thankful. His eyes had started to close, and he was so incredibly hungry. 'We'll ride back, get as clean as we can, eat, then get our heads down. Tomorrow has to be another day!' Aethelstan said finally, and eased his horse around to reverse direction. Even the ride back took energy, which neither of them any longer had, as their gesith realised. Rannulf greeted them with another cauldron of pottage and some venison, which he had thoughtfully held back.

Some of the gerburs were called up to help the brothers from their bloodstained mail. Water appeared. Not particularly hot, but adequate. Rannulf had arranged for a private tent to be erected for the brothers, and once they had wolfed down their food and—wonder of wonders—a little ale, they retired to sleep as if pole-axed.

FOURTEEN

Aethelstan took time to awaken and looked over at Edmund's body, rolled in an animal skin. He saw he still slept. He gave him a gentle kick and Edmund woke with a violent start, for a short while uncertain where he was—then the previous day's horrific events flooded back with a rush.

They had a perfunctory wash, gobbled a little more food then donned cleaned-up chain mail and helmets. Outside two sturdy horses were held and they mounted as Rannulf strode up. He waved ahead and they saw the cart before them.

'I've managed to get some more food cooked up and transported in that cart, sire. It won't stay warm long but it can put a lining in men's bellies. Lucky the Brunanburh villagers forgot it was here,' he explained.

Aethelstan was more impressed than he showed. How many other men would have used their nous in such a manner? Not one in a hundred. Rannulf was now in his local witan, no matter he was still only in his later twenties. His kingdom could never fail with brains like this. When all settled down again he would call another one of his great councils with all local witans present, and he would personally draw everyone's specific attention to this splendid man. How proud Ceorl would have been.

'Excellent!' he praised, and was amused to see Rannulf could still go red-cheeked at an accolade. 'Now we ride,' he nodded to his brother on his right. 'I want Anlaf personally!'

That Rannulf understood only too well, but catching him? He had reservations as to whether his king would succeed, but had enough sense not to air this opinion. He waved then turned to his own hastily arranged tent. He must write a report for Cerdic, Edith and Osburga, and keep it reasonably simple. They could all read but not with his expertise. He eyed three couriers kept waiting nearby. He nodded to one who was very well mounted.

'I'll have an urgent letter to get to Lord Cerdic. You'd better take a two-man escort with you, just in case. This letter has to get through!' he ordered. Quite suddenly he had a flashing vision of his past life when so young.

He was human enough to marvel still at how high he had managed to climb. An earldorman with an estate! Him, Rannulf, born and bred a slave! Now issuing orders that were obeyed on the instant, and he had become a confidant of a king! Had their modern world gone insane? He gave another perplexed shake of his head, entered his tent and prepared to write.

Aethelstan, with Edmund at his side, with a small gesith on guard, moved forward, skirting bodies that still lay around seemingly everywhere. On this second day the slaughter seemed worse. The land stank of death. The earth was stained red. There were still cries for supplication, but fewer than the previous day. Even experienced Aethelstan had never envisaged something like this, and for Edmund it became an education he would never forget. All caused by one obtuse sub-king who obviously thought allies from Dublin would tip the balance. He sighed now. So many good, brave men gone unnecessarily.

Aethelstan let his horse pick his way forward, sitting tight in the saddle when it spooked at the smell of blood. As a pure herd animal, the horse was coiled up, ready to bolt to find others of its kind and away from the hostile stench of blood, which signalled killing predators. The brothers rode with a tight grip, short rein and firm heels for the aids. Each was clad in warlike protection and carried sword and shield, while the bodyguards were armed with spears and javelins. They looked, and were, formidable.

They rode unchallenged though. The enemy had fled or were fleeing as fast as they could. Aethelstan studied each body, but although he did recognise some noble earls, the face for which he hunted was absent.

'Anlaf?' Edmund asked once.

Aethelstan threw him a brief nod. 'He's fled to save his own skin!' and he swore lustily with frustration. 'How I want to face up to him, sword to sword, but I have a feeling it's not to be!' and he cursed again with strong feeling. All long pent-up emotions of the many attempts on his life, when still uncrowned, seethed in him. Only a personal fight could ease such violence, and he rode tight-lipped with a scowl marring his handsome features. They came across Edred, who lay slumped by the decapitated body of Aidan. A medicine woman was with the son who still lived, but with both arms gone. She ignored the royal brothers and threw a simple nod at a warrior escort, who plunged his sword into Edred's chest. Aethelstan pulled another face. They had indeed kept their oaths to him, and he shook his head with genuine sorrow again.

They rode through the morning. The many bodies did thin out at last, but both brothers knew Brunanburh would always carry its own history with this battle name. Then they started to come across walking and stumbling

244

wounded, who stopped to face them with great fear. They could have killed easily but let these men go. Few would live long with some of their wounds. The stinking disease would afflict their bodies, which would turn black, rot, stink and be the preamble to a horrific death when noting could be done for them.

They had left the medicine women long behind. Only the barren land rolled on without vils or even minimal habitation. Edmund cast a look at Aethelstan. 'He's well and truly gone!'

Aethelstan nodded. 'I yearned to meet him above all others, and I have been foiled!' He halted his horse and looked ahead wryly. 'I suppose the sensible thing to do now is go and have a short break with some very special friends of mine. Then I'll call a grand council. It is time you met those who matter. Ha! Who do I see! Pickings good, you old rogue? Some navy captain you've turned out to be, and the man I particularly wanted will be high tailing it on a ship back to Dublin!'

Burhred chuckled. 'I have been ahead of him then, sire, because I split my force again and some of the ships will be lying in wait at sea,' he grinned, flashing his teeth with his wolfish smile.

'If you do get him, don't kill Anlaf. Tie him up and bring him to me—only. That's an order, if you can manage to obey one!' Aethelstan mocked ironically.

'Yes, sire. Of course, sire!' Burhred shot

back, tongue in his cheek, and king and mercenary both knew it.

'Oh get on with you!' Aethelstan said at last, and turned to Edmund. 'You need your wits about you with—him!' he warned jokingly. 'Come on, brother. We'll head back to my second home before we do anything else!'

* * *

Cerdic read Rannulf's latest letter with Edith peering over his shoulder, and Osburga on his other side.

'What a battle it must have been!' Cerdic murmured.

Edith was just so thankful her man was now past it all, and Osburga, reading her mother's mind, threw a tiny nod of agreement.

'He'll be back!' Cerdic announced suddenly. 'He likes to come here to unwind. I bet he'll bring Lord Edmund with him too,' and he turned to Edith, eyebrows raised in silent question.

She pretended to be hurt with ruffled feathers. 'Of course, his chamber is ready and waiting, and the one next will be for Lord Edmund. Just you make sure you have well-mounted scouts out so I can prepare lots of hot water for bathing. As much notice as you can will make life easier!' and she paused. 'He has a great appetite on him and I expect Lord Edmund will be the same. So just you make

246

sure I have roasting meat ready—he likes boar. Get busy and send men out hunting. He could even be here tomorrow or the next day at a pinch!'

Her timescale was uncannily accurate. A fast-riding scout appeared the next evening. 'The king, his brother and some others will be here about noon tomorrow!' he warned, bringing his horse to a slithering halt, where it stood dithering, covered in white foam from a hard gallop. He handed over the reins to a man who took the animal away, then he looked hopefully at the lady of the house. She had a wonderful reputation as a cook.

'I'm hungry, good lady wife!' he said plaintively.

Edith had worked that out. When men came here they were always hungry. Was she the only person who fed them? 'I have strict rules!' she pronounced. 'No one sits at my table until they have washed and in clean clothes. You— smell!' she waved. 'Follow my servant—now! She'll give you hot water and a change of raiment. When I am satisfied, you can eat and not before!' she threatened.

Cerdic turned his head and hissed. 'She's not joking either,' he warned. 'The same rules apply to me too! So move yourself!'

The man did. His nostrils twitched and his mouth filled with saliva. What was that delicious aroma?

Aethelstan smelled roast boar a distance

away, because the wind favoured him. 'Oh! That smell!' he cried and dug his heels further into his mount's flanks. Edmund copied, his own nostrils twitching. What kind of people were these whom his brother king so adored? He was highly intrigued. Although earldormen, they were neither royal nor noble, but he had learned these were one group of genuine people, a close-knit family, where even a king could relax totally and consider them adopted folk. He could put aside the trappings of monarchy and be his own man.

They clattered into a large square, well fortified with an impregnable stockade-type fence, having been waved through by well-armed guards. Servants came to take tired horses away, and Edith and Cerdic greeted them.

Edith was first. 'No, sire. Don't tell me! You are hungry!' she teased. What a likeable man was this king. England was so fortunate. She threw a questioning look at his companion.

Aethelstan remembered his manners. 'My brother Edmund! And he is hungry as well, especially for what we've been smelling the past short distance!' He turned. 'Come, brother. This good lady wife has a specific routine and unless we follow it, we don't eat!' he warned and led the way into the house with a familiarity that amused Edmund.

Later, with stomachs quite full and at ease with life, Aethelstan talked to them as they sat around listening.

Edmund eyed Edith and beamed at her. 'That was a truly wonderful feast.' He rubbed his belly appreciatively then continued. 'Good lady wife. If you were not already married I'd come a-courting you!'

Edith burst into a peal of laughter. 'Sauce!' she chuckled then turned to their king. 'The battle?' she asked, well aware that Cerdic and those who had not been there itched for details.

'It was the mother and father of all battles, and them up there,' and he paused to nod northwards, 'have been bled white. I now have a proper kingdom of England with our English race. I have done what Grandfather Alfred started. In many ways it's tragic so many good men have had to die, but I suppose it was inevitable. If I have one true regret it's that I wasn't able to kill Anlaf personally.'

'Burhred?' Cerdic asked.

'He was there as well. Left someone in charge of the ships and rode like a madman to join in, but was too late. Except for the pickings afterwards. He's a good man when he decides to obey orders!' he grinned. 'As for you, young man,' he faced Rannulf. 'You excelled yourself. Arranging food like you did was sheer genius. Many others died. Hoel was pretty badly wounded in his right arm. Whether he'll ever be able to use it again properly is a moot point. Aidan and Edred died fighting together. They were two good men as well and my gesith numbers have been thinned drastically. We two were lucky,' and he nodded at Edmund who sat quietly but missed not a word or gesture.

'We really are at peace, sire?' Osburga asked quietly. With two children this knowledge was important.

'Yes!' Aethelstan said firmly. 'I saw your old friend Judith. She has acquired a companion,' and he explained in detail, then turned to Cerdic. 'I wish to call a grand council, to put everyone in the picture. Arrange this please. It can be at Tamworth I think, and all visitors and scholars can attend as well.'

'I could manage to ride there if I left in advance,' Cerdic told him.

Aethelstan eyed him dubiously, and also saw Edith's frown. He hastened to nip any marital row in the bud. 'All of you come!' he invited. 'A party can leave in advance, and then we will have our *own* party of celebration for the founding of us English and the consolidation of our boundaries. Now how about that?' he beamed at them all.

There was a subdued murmuring from Edith and Osburga. 'But what about me?' Osburga protested, feeling completely left out.

Edith hastened to soothe ruffled feathers there. 'We have some wonderful house servants. They can have a change and look after the children!'

250

Osburga thought for just two heartbeats then nodded enthusiastically and chuckled at Rannulf. 'You men are not going to have all the fun to yourselves!'

Aethelstan let out a sigh of relief. Being faced by two irate ladies would ruin this good day. He lifted his tankard, drained it in one swallow and waited until it was refilled. He lifted it high, aware every eye was on him.

'Come, my dear friends! Lift your tankards and drink with me—to THE BIRTH OF THE ENGLISH in this wonderful year of 937.

THE END

HISTORY

Two years later in 939 Aethelstan was dead and Edmund became King. Aethelstan was born in 895 and was only forty-four years when he died. He had been king from 924 to 939, a very short reign, but he did so much in it. He is recognised as the first king of all the English, but of what he died we simply do not know. It may have been something like leukaemia, cancer of the blood, which then was totally unknown. Or it could have been some genetic defect inherited from King Alfred's family line. Doctors today think Alfred, who was ill throughout his life, may have suffered from a condition like Crohn's disease. Because of this, it is astonishing what Alfred did manage to accomplish, with his laws, education, languages, foreign allies as well as fighting. Whether he did burn the housewife's cakes is a charming story handed down to us but a man with so much on his mind could be forgiven for his daydreaming.

Aethelstan was Alfred's illegitimate grandson and, like his grandfather, Aethelflaeda the Lady of Mercia as well as his own father, he died young. Perhaps there was a genetic defect in Alfred's family that had to be bred out over the generations. It is impossible to find details. The records stay silent.

Historians who read what is a novel may carp that it lacks dates, except for the great battle. The reason is that the few records that are available all contradict themselves. It is considered even the great *Anglo-Saxon Chronicle* was written after Aethelstan's death during Edmund's reign. Aethelstan died at Gloucester but was buried at Malmesbury, a place much loved by him.

The many attempts to kill Aethelstan before his crowning did take place, but again no details are to hand, so I have used a writer's licence, except concerning the bishop's murder when staying in the king's tent. Aethelstan was warned, but by a soldier who did recognise Anlaf. Once more I have changed this to the scribe for the story's sake.

Some of the old records talk about a famous scribe known simply as Aethelstan A. I have changed this to Rannulf. As to the other death attempts I have had to use my imagination and logic.

Where was Brunanburh? We do not know even in this twenty-first century. Historians all argue furiously. Disagreeing in the process. I studied the map, took into account the type of land and the limited transport then to hand and again used my mind. It is reasonable to assume that if people did move back after the battle, Brunanburh may have simply been one of those places that vanished during the plagues, when not enough living were left to bury the dead and Nature simply took over. Perhaps one day some company may dig a deep trench for, say, a gas pipeline, and remains and artefacts will be found that can be accurately dated to 937. One thing is agreed. Brunanburh was the greatest, longest, bloodiest battle to have taken place on this island. Yet it appears to have been airbrushed from history. Year 1066 and Hastings were almost a kindergarten affair in comparison.

Aethelstan died satisfied at the England he had made, but not long after his death there were fresh troubles. Edmund even lost part of his land but fought and regained it. This trouble went on even with the great Canute. It was William first who stopped it by the simple expedient of building huge stone castles, filling them with warriors and, at the same time, dispossessing the Saxon nobility. He gave their estates to the followers who had come over with him. In the process many noble Saxons were reduced to penury.

Edmund was a very good and popular king. On 26th May 946, when just twenty-five years, he was murdered about eight miles from where I sit and write this book at Pucklechurch, South Gloucestershire.

It took place at the Royal Saxon Palace when Edmund and his men were celebrating St Augustine's Day Mass.

Present at the king's table was Leofa, a robber who had already been banned. There was a violent altercation between Leofa and the king's cupbearer. Edmund walked down to see what it was all about. Leofa drew his knife and may just have meant to kill the cupbearer. The king though stepped in the way and the knife went into him. It must have gone straight into Edmund's aorta, which was very fatal. The blood gushed from him and he died on the spot.

There are two endings to this story, neither of which can be proved. The first goes that the guards rushed down and likewise killed Leofa, but this is unlikely. They would be full of drink and frozen with shock at Edmund's killing. Leofa had not been drinking so long. He leaped to his feet, rushed outside, grabbed a horse and escaped. He would then become an outlaw when any man, woman or even child would be free to kill him for his regicide. I think this is the most likely event, though he would not live long. In our cold, wet winters he would be worse off than the wild animals, who had their snug dens and knew exactly how to cope with the cold months. What life there was left to Leofa would be quite miserable. And that is all history has to say about him.

The street of meat Fleshammels is today's famous Shambles at York, and the wide windows still show from where meat was sold. The old English name for York was Fofbrwic, which meant meats-wild-boar-town. The old Norse name of Yorvik translated to mean

Horse Bay. At York in this twenty-first century there is so much to see, do and admire as well as find history on every side.

Judith was one of the ancient healing women thought to go right back to the Druids. They had a potent interest in the future and were right more than wrong. These usually became the unfortunates, centuries later, who were branded as witches and burned at the stake.

At Yate in South Gloucestershire there is a large school called King Edmund's, now an academy, so he is well remembered.

The Anglo-Saxon Chronicle says:–

Five Kings lay on the field of battle
In bloom of youth, pierced with swords
So seven eke of the Earls of Anlaf
And of the ships' crews, unnumbered
   crowds
There was dispersed the little band
Of hardy Scots. The dread of Northern
   hordes
The Northmen sailed in their nailed ships
Urged to the noisy deep by unrelenting fate
A dreary remnant on the roaring sea
Over deep waters, Dublin they sought
And Ireland's shores in deep disgrace.

Alfred, Lord Tennyson, translated the whole of the *Chronicle* and here are two relevant sections:

Five young Kings put asleep by the sword
    stroke
Seven strong Earls of the army of Anlaf
Fell on the Warfield, numberless numbers
Shipmen and Scotsmen.

There are many verses beautifully translated
that start with:–

Aethelstan King
Lord among Earls
Bracelet bestower and
Baron of Barons
He with his brother
Edmund Atheling
Gaining a lifelong
Glory in battle
Slew with the sword edge
There by Brunanburh
Brake the shield wall
Hew'd the Lindenwood
Hack'd the battle shield
Sons of Edward with hammered brands.